Christmas Ghosts

Christmas Ghosts

An Anthology Selected
by Seon Manley and Gogo Lewis

DOUBLEDAY & COMPANY, INC.
GARDEN CITY, NEW YORK

ACM

Library of Congress Cataloging in Publication Data
Main entry under title:

Christmas ghosts.

CONTENTS: Bowen, M. The prescription.—Allingham,
M. On Christmas Day in the morning.—Lord Dunsany.
Thirteen at table. [etc.]
1. Ghost stories, English.   2. Christmas stories.
I. Manley, Seon.   II. Lewis, Gogo.
PZ1.C463   [PR1309.G5]   823'.01
ISBN 0-385-14032-0 Trade
0-385-14033-9 Prebound
Library of Congress Catalog Card Number 77–26517

This book is for our families
with love

Acknowledgments

We are grateful to the authors, agents, and publishers who have given us permission to reprint the following selections.

"The Prescription" from *The Last Bouquet* by Marjorie Bowen. Reprinted by permission of Kirby McCauley, Ltd.

"On Christmas Day in the Morning" from *The Mysterious Mr. Campion* by Margery Allingham. Copyright © 1963 by P. & M. Youngman Carter Ltd. Reprinted by permission of Paul R. Reynolds, Inc. 599 Fifth Avenue, New York, N.Y. 10017.

"Thirteen at Table" from *Tales of Wonder* by Lord Dunsany. Reprinted by permission of Curtis Brown Ltd. on behalf of the Estate of Lord Dunsany.

"Tarnhelm" by Hugh Walpole. Reprinted by permission of Rupert Hart-Davis.

"Transition" from *Tales of the Mysterious and Macabre* by Algernon Blackwood. Reprinted by permission of The Public Trustee and the Hamlyn Group Ltd.

"The Ether Hogs" from *Two Trifles* by Oliver Onions. Reprinted by permission of Miss Berta Ruck.

"The White Road" by E. F. Bozman from *Ghost Stories* selected and introduced by John Hampden. An Everyman's Library Edition. Published in the United States by E. P. Dutton, and reprinted with their permission. Also reprinted by permission of J. M. Dent & Sons Ltd.

"The Necklace of Pearls" from *Lord Peter* by Dorothy L. Sayers. Copyright © 1933 by Dorothy Leigh Sayers Fleming, renewed 1961 by Lloyds Bank Ltd., Executors. Reprinted by permission of Harper & Row, Publishers, Inc.

Our thanks also to Jane Kendall; Betty Shalders; the staff of the Bellport Memorial Library, Bellport, New York; the staff of the Patchogue Library, Patchogue, New York; the staff of the Greenwich Library, Greenwich, Connecticut.

Contents

Introduction

"There is probably a smell of roasted chestnuts and other good comfortable things all the time, for we are telling Winter stories—Ghost stories, or more shame for us—round the Christmas fire; and we have never stirred except to draw a little nearer to it."

So said that old literary Father Christmas himself, Charles Dickens. Ghost stories, mysterious stories, weird stories—those have been the stuff of tales since the human family first celebrated the holidays of the winter solstice.

This is a collection of deliciously scary fare for the Christmas season . . . that time when, in more primitive worlds, ghosts walked so frequently that the animals had to talk and the cocks to crow just to hold the spectral at bay. On this ancient primitive fear a whole literature has been built up. These Christmas tales were best sellers in the magazines and old holiday keepsakes of yesteryear. The annual Christmas ghost story reached its crowning glory with the work of Charles Dickens. The Christmas season still inspires twentieth-century writers, and there is a new supernatural delight in mysterious spectral Christmas tales.

So here for your pleasure are great ghosts and great reading for great holidays.

SEON MANLEY
GOGO LEWIS

The Prescription

MARJORIE BOWEN

*Oh, those great Christmases of old! The wassail bowls,
good round bowls circled with ribbons, the great plum
puddings, the Christmas pies, the geese, the turkeys, the
carols, the reddened cheeks, snow on the ground. Oh,
Christmas was Christmas then! Every generation main-
tains that Christmas past was always better.*

*Marjorie Bowen, whose life spanned the nineteenth
and twentieth centuries, knew this to be nonsense. The
best Christmas is always now—and the best type of
story for Christmas Eve . . . ? Well, a ghost story.*

*Here, Gabrielle Margaret Long, who wrote under
the names of Marjorie Bowen, George R. Preedy, and
Joseph Shearing, gives us an appropriate prescription
for the uncanny. Our contemporary Graham Greene
found her such a perfect tonic that she inspired all his
early writings.*

JOHN CUMING collected ghost stories; he always declared that this was the best that he knew, although it was partially secondhand and contained a mystery that had no reasonable solution, while most really good ghost stories allow of a plausible explanation, even if it is one as feeble as a dream, excusing all; or a hallucination or a crude deception. Cuming told the story rather well. The first part of it at least had come under his own observation and been carefully noted by him in the flat green book which he kept for the record of all curious cases of this sort. He was a shrewd and trained observer; he honestly restrained his love of drama from leading him into embellishing facts. Cuming told the story to us all on the most suitable occasion—Christmas Eve—and prefaced it with a little homily.

"You all know the good old saw—'The more it changes the more it is the same thing'—and I should like you to notice that this extremely up-to-date ultramodern ghost story is really almost exactly the same as one that might have puzzled Babylonian or Assyrian sages. I can give you the first start of the tale in my own words, but the second part will have to be in the words of someone else. They were, however, most carefully and scrupulously taken down. As for the conclusion, I must leave you to draw that for yourselves—each according to your own mood, fancy, and temperament; it may be that you will all think of the same solution, it may be that you will each think of a different one, and it may be that everyone will be left wondering."

Having thus enjoyed himself by whetting our curiosity, Cuming settled himself down comfortably in his deep armchair and unfolded his tale.

"It was about five years ago. I don't wish to be exact
with time, and of course I shall alter names—that's one
of the first rules of the game, isn't it? Well, whenever it
was, I was the guest of a—Mrs. Janey we will call her
—who was, to some extent, a friend of mine; an intelligent, lively, rather bustling sort of woman who had the
knack of gathering interesting people about her. She
had lately taken a new house in Buckinghamshire. It
stood in the grounds of one of those large estates which
are now so frequently being broken up. She was very
pleased with the house, which was quite new and had
only been finished a year, and seemed, according to her
own rather excited imagination, in every way desirable.
I don't want to emphasize anything about the house except that it was new and did stand on the verge, as it
were, of this large old estate, which had belonged to
one of those notable English families now extinct and
completely forgotten. I am no antiquarian or connois-
seur in architecture, and the rather blatant modernity
of the house did not offend me. I was able to appreciate
its comfort and to enjoy what Mrs. Janey rather mad-
deningly called 'the old-world gardens,' which were really a section of the larger gardens of the vanished
mansion which had once commanded this domain.
Mrs. Janey, I should tell you, knew nothing about the
neighborhood nor anyone who lived there, except that
for the first it was very convenient for town, and for the
second she believed that they were all 'nice' people, not
likely to bother one. I was slightly disappointed with
the crowd she had gathered together at Christmas.
They were all people whom either I knew too well or
whom I didn't wish to know at all, and at first the

party showed signs of being extremely flat. Mrs. Janey
seemed to perceive this too, and with rather nervous
haste produced, on Christmas Eve, a trump card in the
way of amusement—a professional medium, called
Mrs. Mahogany, because that could not possibly have
been her name. Some of us 'believed in,' as the saying
goes, mediums, and some didn't; but we were all willing to be diverted by the experiment. Mrs. Janey continually lamented that a certain Dr. Dilke would not be
present. He was going to be one of the party, but had
been detained in town and would not reach Verrall,
which was the name of the house, until later, and the
medium, it seemed, could not stay; for she, being a per-
sonage in great demand, must go on to a further engagement. I, of course, like everyone else possessed of
an intelligent curiosity and a certain amount of leisure,
had been to mediums before. I had been slightly
impressed, slightly disgusted, and very much bewildered, and on the whole had decided to let the matter
alone, considering that I really preferred the more direct and old-fashioned method of getting in touch with
what we used to call 'The Unseen.' This sitting in the
great new house seemed rather banal. I could understand in some haunted old manor that a clairvoyant, or
a clairaudient, or a trance-medium might have found
something interesting to say, but what was she going to
get out of Mrs. Janey's bright, brilliant, and comfortable dwelling?

"Mrs. Mahogany was a nondescript sort of woman—
neither young nor old, neither clever nor stupid, neither
dark nor fair, placid, and not in the least self-conscious.
After an extremely good luncheon (it was a gloomy,

stormy afternoon) we all sat down in a circle in the
cheerful drawing room; the curtains were pulled across
the dreary prospect of gray sky and gray landscape,
and we had merely the light of the fire. We sat quite
close together in order to increase 'the power,' as Mrs.
Mahogany said, and the medium sat in the middle,
with no special precautions against trickery; but we all
knew that trickery would have been really impossible,
and we were quite prepared to be tremendously
impressed and startled if any manifestations took place.
I think we all felt rather foolish, as we did not know
each other very well, sitting round there, staring at this
very ordinary, rather common, stout little woman, who
kept nervously pulling a little tippet of gray wool over
her shoulders, closing her eyes and muttering, while she
twisted her fingers together. When we had sat silent for
about ten minutes Mrs. Janey announced in a rather
raw whisper that the medium had gone into a trance.
'Beautifully,' she added. I thought that Mrs. Mahogany did not look at all beautiful. Her communication
began with a lot of rambling talk which had no point at
all, and a good deal of generalization under which I
think we all became a little restive. There was too
much of various spirits who had all sorts of ordinary
names, just regular Toms, Dicks, and Harrys of the
spirit world, floating round behind us, their arms full of
flowers and their mouths of good will, all rather point-
less. And though, occasionally, a Tom, a Dick, or a
Harry was identified by some of us, it wasn't very convincing, and, what was worse, not very interesting. We
got, however, our surprise and our shock, because Mrs.
Mahogany began suddenly to writhe into ugly contor-

tions and called out in a loud voice, quite different from
the one that she had hitherto used: 'Murder!'

"This word gave us all a little thrill, and we leaned
forward eagerly to hear what further she had to say.
With every sign of distress and horror Mrs. Mahogany
began to speak:

"'He's murdered her. Oh, how dreadful. Look at
him! Can't somebody stop him? It's so near here, too.
He tried to save her. He was sorry, you know. Oh, how
dreadful! Look at him—he's borne it as long as he can,
and now he's murdered her! I see him mixing it in a
glass. Oh, isn't it awful that no one could have saved
her—and he was so terribly remorseful afterward. Oh,
how dreadful! How horrible!'

"She ended in a whimpering of fright and horror,
and Mrs. Janey, who seemed an adept at this sort of
thing, leaned forward and asked eagerly:

"'Can't you get the name—can't you find out who
it is? Why do you get that here?'

"'I don't know,' muttered the medium, 'it's somewhere near here—a house, an old dark house, and
there are curtains of mauve velvet—do you call it
mauve? a kind of blue red—at the windows. There's a
garden outside with a fishpond and you go through a
low doorway and down stone steps.'

"'It isn't near here,' said Mrs. Janey decidedly, 'all
the houses are new.'

"'The house is near here,' persisted the medium. 'I
am walking through it now; I can see the room, I can
see that poor, poor woman, and a glass of milk——'

"'I wish you'd get the name,' insisted Mrs. Janey,
and she cast a look, as I thought not without suspicion,

round the circle. 'You can't be getting this from my house, you know, Mrs. Mahogany,' she added decidedly, 'it must be given out by someone here—something they've read or seen, you know,' she said, to reassure us that our characters were not in dispute.

"But the medium replied drowsily, 'No, it's somewhere near here. I see a light dress covered with small roses. If he could have got help he would have gone for it, but there was no one; so all his remorse was useless. . . .'

"No further urging would induce the medium to say more; soon afterward she came out of the trance, and all of us, I think, felt that she had made rather a stupid blunder by introducing this vague piece of melodrama, and if it was, as we suspected, a cheap attempt to give a ghostly and mysterious atmosphere to Christmas Eve, it was a failure.

"When Mrs. Mahogany, blinking round her, said brightly, 'Well, here I am again! I wonder if I said anything that interested you?' we all replied rather coldly, 'Of course it has been most interesting, but there hasn't been anything definite.' And I think that even Mrs. Janey felt that the sitting had been rather a disappointment, and she suggested that if the weather was really too horrible to venture out of doors we should sit round the fire and tell old-fashioned ghost stories. 'The kind,' she said brightly, 'that are about bones and chairs and shrouds. I really think that is the most thrilling kind after all.' Then, with some embarrassment, and when Mrs. Mahogany had left the room, she suggested that not one of us should say anything about what the medium had said in her trance.

" 'It really was rather absurd,' said our hostess, 'and it would make me look a little foolish if it got about; you know some people think these mediums are absolute fakes, and anyhow, the whole thing, I am afraid, was quite stupid. She must have got her contacts mixed. There is no old house about here and never has been since the original Verrall was pulled down, and that's a good fifty years ago, I believe, from what the estate agent told me; and as for a murder, I never heard the shadow of any such story.'

"We all agreed not to mention what the medium had said, and did this with the more heartiness as we were, not any one of us, impressed. The feeling was rather that Mrs. Mahogany had been obliged to say something and had said that. . . .

"Well," said Cuming comfortably, "that is the first part of my story, and I daresay you'll think it's dull enough. Now we come to the second part.

"Latish that evening Dr. Dilke arrived. He was not in any way a remarkable man, just an ordinary successful physician, and I refuse to say that he was suffering from overwork or nervous strain; you know that is so often put into this kind of story as a sort of excuse for what happens afterward. On the contrary, Dr. Dilke seemed to be in the most robust of health and the most cheerful frame of mind, and quite prepared to make the most of his brief holiday. The car that fetched him from the station was taking Mrs. Mahogany away, and the doctor and the medium met for just a moment in the hall. Mrs. Janey did not trouble to introduce them, but without waiting for this Mrs. Mahogany turned to the doctor, and looking at him fixedly, said, 'You're very psychic, aren't you?' And upon that Mrs. Janey was forced to say hastily: 'This is Mrs. Mahogany, Dr. Dilke, the famous medium.'

"The physician was indifferently impressed. 'I really don't know,' he answered, smiling, 'I have never gone in for that sort of thing. I shouldn't think I am what you call "psychic" really; I have had a hard, scientific training, and that rather knocks the bottom out of fantasies.'

"'Well, you are, you know,' said Mrs. Mahogany; 'I felt it at once; I shouldn't be at all surprised if you had some strange experience one of these days.'

"Mrs. Mahogany left the house and was duly driven away to the station. I want to make the point very clear that she and Dr. Dilke did not meet again and that they held no communication except those few words in the hall spoken in the presence of Mrs. Janey. Of course Dr. Dilke got twitted a good deal about what the medium had said; it made quite a topic of conversation during dinner and after dinner, and we all had queer little ghost stories or incidents of what we considered 'psychic' experiences to trot out and discuss. Dr. Dilke remained civil, amused, but entirely unconvinced. He had what he called a material, or physical, or medical explanation for almost everything that we said, and, apart from all these explanations he added, with some justice, that human credulity was such that there was always someone who would accept and embellish anything, however wild, unlikely, or grotesque it was.

"'I should rather like to hear what you would say if such an experience happened to you,' Mrs. Janey challenged him; 'whether you use the ancient terms of "ghost," "witches," "black magic," and so on, or whether you speak in modern terms like "medium," "clairvoyance," "psychic contacts," and all the rest of it; well, it seems one is in a bit of a tangle anyhow, and if any queer thing ever happens to you——'

"Dr. Dilke broke in pleasantly: 'Well, if it ever does I will let you all know about it, and I dare say I shall have an explanation to add at the end of the tale.'

"When we all met again the next morning we rather hoped that Dr. Dilke *would* have something to tell us— some odd experience that might have befallen him in the night, new as the house was, and banal as was his bedroom. He told us, of course, that he had passed a perfectly good night.

"We most of us went to the morning service in the small church that had once been the chapel belonging to the demolished mansion, and which had some rather curious monuments inside and in the churchyard. As I went in I noticed a mortuary chapel with niches for the coffins to be stood upright, now whitewashed and used as a sacristy. The monuments and mural tablets were mostly to the memory of members of the family of Verrall—the Verralls of Verrall Hall, who appeared to have been people of little interest or distinction. Dr. Dilke sat beside me, and I, having nothing better to do through the more familiar and monotonous portions of the service, found myself idly looking at the mural tablet beyond him. This was a large slab of black marble deeply cut with a very worn Latin inscription which I found, unconsciously, I was spelling out. The stone, it seemed, commemorated a woman who had been, of course, the possessor of all the virtues; her name was Philadelphia Carwithen, and I rather pleasantly sampled the flavor of that ancient name—Philadelphia. Then I noticed a smaller inscription at the bottom of the slab, which indicated that the lady's husband also rested in the vault; he had died suddenly about six months after her—of grief at her loss, I thought, scenting out a pretty romance.

"As we walked home across the frost-bitten fields and icy lanes Dr. Dilke, who walked beside me, as he had sat beside me in church, began to complain of cold; he said he believed that he had caught a chill. I was rather amused to hear this old-womanish expression on the lips of so distinguished a physician, and I told him that I had been taught in my more enlightened days that there was no such thing as 'catching a chill.' To my surprise he did not laugh at this, but said:

" 'Oh, yes, there is, and I believe I've got it—I keep on shivering: I think it was that slab of black stone I was sitting next. It was as cold as ice, for I touched it, and it seemed to me exuding moisture—some of that old stone does, you know; it's always, as it were, sweating; and I felt exactly as if I were sitting next a slab of ice from which a cold wind was blowing; it was really as if it penetrated my flesh.'

"He looked pale, and I thought how disagreeable it would be for us all, and particularly for Mrs. Janey, if the good man was to be taken ill in the midst of her already not-too-successful Christmas party. Dr. Dilke seemed, too, in that ill-humor which so often presages an illness; he was quite peevish about the church and the service, and the fact that he had been asked to go there.

"'These places are nothing but charnel houses, after all,' he said fretfully; 'one sits there among all those rotting bones, with that damp marble at one's side. . . .'

"'It is supposed to give you "atmosphere,"' I said. 'The atmosphere of an old-fashioned Christmas. . . . Did you notice who your black stone was erected "to the memory of"?' I asked, and the doctor replied that he had not.

"'It was to a young woman—a young woman, I took it, and her husband: "Philadelphia Carwithen," I noticed that, and of course there was a long eulogy of her virtues, and then underneath it just said that he had died a few months afterward. As far as I could see it was the only example of that name in the church—all the rest were Verralls. I suppose they were strangers here.'

"'What was the date?' asked the doctor, and I replied that really I had not been able to make it out, for where the Roman figures came the stone had been very worn.

"The day ambled along somehow, with games, diversions, and plenty of good food and drink, and toward the evening we began to feel a little more satisfied with each other and our hostess. Only Dr. Dilke remained a little peevish and apart, and this was remarkable in one who was obviously of a robust temperament and an even temper. He still continued to talk of a 'chill,' and I did notice that he shuddered once or twice, and continually sat near the large fire which Mrs. Janey had rather laboriously arranged in imitation of what she would call 'the good old times.'

"That evening, the evening of Christmas Day, there was no talk whatever of ghosts or psychic matters; our discussions were entirely topical and of mundane matters, in which Dr. Dilke, who seemed to have recovered his spirits, took his part with ability and agreeableness. When it was time to break up I asked him, half in jest, about his mysterious chill, and he looked at me with some surprise and appeared to have forgotten that he had ever said he had got such a thing; the impression, whatever it was, which he had received in the church, had evidently been effaced from his mind. I wish to make that quite clear.

"The next morning Dr. Dilke appeared very late at the breakfast table, and when he did so his looks were a matter for hints and comment; he was pale, distracted, troubled, untidy in his dress, absent in his manner, and I, at least, instantly recalled what he had said yesterday, and feared he was sickening for some illness.

"On Mrs. Janey putting to him some direct question as to his looks and manner, so strange and so troubled, he replied rather sharply, 'Well, I don't know what you can expect from a fellow who's been up all night. I thought I came down here for a rest.'

"We all looked at him as he dropped into his place and began to drink his coffee with eager gusto; I noticed that he continually shivered. There was something about this astounding statement and his curious appearance which held us all discreetly silent. We waited for further developments before committing

ourselves; even Mrs. Janey, whom I had never thought
of as tactful, contrived to say casually:

" 'Up all night, doctor. Couldn't you sleep, then? I'm
so sorry if your bed wasn't comfortable.'

" 'The bed was all right,' he answered, 'that made
me the more sorry to leave it. Haven't you got a local
doctor who can take the local cases?' he added.

" 'Why, of course we have; there's Dr. Armstrong
and Dr. Fraser—I made sure about that before I came
here.'

" 'Well, then,' demanded Dr. Dilke angrily, 'why on
earth couldn't one of them have gone last night?'

"Mrs. Janey looked at me helplessly, and I, obeying
her glance, took up the matter.

" 'What do you mean, doctor? Do you mean that you
were called out of your bed last night to attend a case?'
I asked deliberately.

" 'Of course I was—I only got back with the dawn.'

"Here Mrs. Janey could not forbear breaking in.

" 'But whoever could it have been? I know nobody
about here yet, at least, only one or two people by
name, and they would not be aware that you were here.
And how did you get out of the house? It's locked every
night.'

"Then the doctor gave his story in rather, I must
confess, a confused fashion, and yet with an earnest
conviction that he was speaking the simple truth. It
was broken up a good deal by ejaculations and com-
ments from the rest of us, but I give it you here shorn of
all that and exactly as I put it down in my notebook afterward.

" 'I was awakened by a tap at the door. I was in-

stantly wide-awake and I said, "Come in." I thought
immediately that probably someone in the house was ill
—a doctor, you know, is always ready for these emer-
gencies. The door opened at once, and a man entered
holding a small ordinary storm-lantern. I noticed nothing peculiar about the man. He had a dark greatcoat
on, and appeared extremely anxious. "I am sorry to disturb you," he said at once, "but there is a young woman
dangerously ill. I want you to come and see her." I,
somehow, did not think of arguing or of suggesting that
there were other medical men in the neighborhood, or
of asking how it was he knew of my presence at Verrall.
I dressed myself quickly and accompanied him out of
the house. He opened the front door without any trouble, and it did not occur to me to ask him how it was he
had obtained either admission or egress. There was a
small carriage outside the door, such a one as you may
still see in isolated country places, but such a one as I
was certainly surprised to see here. I could not very
well make out either the horse or the driver, for,
though the moon was high in the heavens, it was frequently obscured by clouds. I got into the carriage and
noticed, as I have often noticed before in these ancient
vehicles, a most repulsive smell of decay and damp. My
companion got in beside me. He did not speak a word
during the whole of the journey, which was, I have the
impression, extremely long. I had also the sense that he
was in the greatest trouble, anguish, and almost de-
spair; I do not know why I did not question him. I
should tell you that he had drawn down the blinds of
the carriage and we traveled in darkness, yet I was perfectly aware of his presence and seemed to see him in

his heavy dark greatcoat turned up round the chin, his
black hair low on his forehead, and his anxious, furtive
dark eyes. I think I may have gone to sleep in the carriage, I was tired and cold. I was aware, however, when
it stopped, and of my companion opening the door and
helping me out. We went through a garden, down some
steps and past a fishpond; I could see by the moonlight
the silver and gold shapes of fishes slipping in and out
of the black water. We entered the house by a side door
—I remember that very distinctly—and went up what
seemed to be some secret or seldom-used stairs, and into
a bedroom. I was, by now, quite alert, as one is when
one gets into the presence of the patient, and said to
myself, "What a fool I've been, I've brought nothing
with me," and I tried to remember, but could not quite
do so, whether or not I had brought anything with me
—my cases and so on—to Verrall. The room was very
badly lighted, but a certain illumination—I could not
say whether it came from any artificial light within the
room or merely from the moonlight through the open
window, draped with mauve velvet curtains—fell on
the bed, and there I saw my patient. She was a young
woman, who, I surmised, would have been, when in
health, of considerable though coarse charm. She was
now in great suffering, twisted and contorted with
agony, and in her struggles of anguish had pulled and
torn the bedclothes into a heap. I noticed that she wore
a dress of some light material spotted with small roses,
and it occurred to me at once that she had been taken
ill during the daytime and must have lain thus in great
pain for many hours, and I turned with some reproach
to the man who had fetched me and demanded why

help had not been sought sooner. For answer he wrung his hands—a gesture that I do not remember having noticed in any human being before; one hears a great deal of hands being wrung, but one does not so often see it. This man, I remember distinctly, wrung his hands, and muttered, "Do what you can for her—do what you can!" I feared that this would be very little. I endeavored to make an examination of the patient, but owing to her half-delirious struggles this was very difficult; she was, however, I thought, likely to die, and of what malady I could not determine. There was a table near by on which lay some papers—one I took to be a will—and a glass in which there had been milk. I do not remember seeing anything else in the room—the light was so bad. I endeavored to question the man, whom I took to be the husband, but without any success. He merely repeated his monotonous appeal for me to save her. Then I was aware of a sound outside the room—of a woman laughing, perpetually and shrilly laughing. "Pray stop that," I cried to the man; "who have you got in the house—a lunatic?" But he took no notice of my appeal, merely repeating his own hushed lamentations. The sick woman appeared to hear that demoniacal laughter outside, and raising herself on one elbow said, "You have destroyed me and you may well laugh."

"'I sat down at the table on which were the papers and the glass half full of milk, and wrote a prescription on a sheet torn out of my notebook. The man snatched it eagerly. "I don't know when and where you can get that made up," I said, "but it's the only hope." At this he seemed wishful for me to depart, as wishful as he

had been for me to come. "That's all I want," he said.
He took me by the arm and led me out of the house by
the same back stairs. As I descended I still heard those
two dreadful sounds—the thin laughter of the woman I
had not seen, and the groans, becoming every moment
fainter, of the young woman whom I had seen. The
carriage was waiting for me, and I was driven back by
the same way I had come. When I reached the house
and my room I saw the dawn just breaking. I rested till
I heard the breakfast gong. I suppose some time had
gone by since I returned to the house, but I wasn't quite
aware of it; all through the night I had rather lost the
sense of time.'

   "When Dr. Dilke had finished his narrative, which I
give here badly—but, I hope, to the point—we all
glanced at each other rather uncomfortably, for who
was to tell a man like Dr. Dilke that he had been suffering from severe hallucination? It was, of course, quite
impossible that he could have left the house and gone
through the peculiar scenes he had described, and it
seemed extraordinary that he could for a moment have
believed that he had done so. What was even more remarkable was that so many points of his story agreed
with what the medium, Mrs. Mahogany, had said in
her trance. We recognized the frock with the roses,
the mauve velvet curtains, the glass of milk, the man
who had fetched Dr. Dilke sounded like the murderer,
and the unfortunate woman writhing on the bed
sounded like the victim; but how had the doctor got
hold of these particulars? We all knew that he had not
spoken to Mrs. Mahogany, and each suspected the
other of having told him what the medium had said,

and that this having wrought on his mind he had the
dream, vision, or hallucination he had just described to
us. I must add that this was found afterward to be
wholly false; we were all reliable people and there was
not a shadow of doubt we had all kept our counsel about
Mrs. Mahogany. In fact, none of us had been alone
with Dr. Dilke the previous day for more than a moment or so save myself, who had walked with him from
the church, when we had certainly spoken of nothing
except the black stone in the church and the chill
which he had said emanated from it. . . . Well, to put
the matter as briefly as possible, and to leave out a
great deal of amazement and wonder, explanation, and
so on, we will come to the point when Dr. Dilke was
finally persuaded that he had not left Verrall all the
night. When his story was taken to pieces and put before him, as it were, in the raw, he himself recognized
many absurdities: How could the man have come
straight to his bedroom? How could he have left the
house?—the doors were locked every night, there was
no doubt about that. Where did the carriage come
from and where was the house to which he had been
taken? And who could possibly have known of his presence in the neighborhood? Had not, too, the scene in
the house to which he was taken all the resemblance of
a nightmare? Who was it laughing in the other room?
What was the mysterious illness that was destroying the
young woman? Who was the black-browed man who
had fetched him? And, in these days of telephone and
motorcars, people didn't go out in the old-fashioned
one-horse carriages to fetch doctors from miles away in
the case of dangerous illness.

"Dr. Dilke was finally silenced, uneasy, but not convinced. I could see that he disliked intensely the idea that he had been the victim of a hallucination and that he equally intensely regretted the impulse which had made him relate his extraordinary adventure of the night. I could only conclude that he must have done so while still, to an extent, under the influence of his delusion, which had been so strong that never for a moment had he questioned the reality of it. Though he was forced at last to allow us to put the whole thing down as a most remarkable dream, I could see that he did not intend to let the matter rest there, and later in the day (out of good manners we had eventually ceased discussing the story) he asked me if I would accompany him on some investigation in the neighborhood.

" 'I think I should know the house,' he said, 'even though I saw it in the dark. I was impressed by the fishpond and the low doorway through which I had to stoop in order to pass without knocking my head.'

"I did not tell him that Mrs. Mahogany had also mentioned a fishpond and a low door.

"We made the excuse of some old brasses we wished to discover in a near-by church to take my car and go out that afternoon on an investigation of the neighborhood in the hope of discovering Dr. Dilke's dream house.

"We covered a good deal of distance and spent a good deal of time without any success at all, and the short day was already darkening when we came upon a row of almshouses in which, for no reason at all that I could discern, Dr. Dilke showed an interest and insisted on stopping before them. He pointed out an inscription cut in the center gable, which said that these had been built by a certain Richard Carwithen in memory of Philadelphia, his wife.

"'The people whose tablet you sat next in the church,' I remarked.

"'Yes,' murmured Dr. Dilke, 'when I felt the chill,' and he added, 'when I *first* felt the chill. You see, the date is 1830. That would be about right.'

"We stopped in the little village, which was a good many miles from Verrall, and after some tedious delays because everything was shut up for the holiday, we did discover an old man who was willing to tell us something about the almshouses, though there was nothing much to be said about them. They had been founded by a certain Mr. Richard Carwithen with his wife's fortune. He had been a poor man, a kind of adventurer, our informant thought, who had married a wealthy woman; they had not been at all happy. There had been quarrels and disputes, and a separation (at least, so the gossip went, as his father had told it to him); finally, the Carwithens had taken a house here in this village of Sunford—a large house it was and it still stood. The Carwithens weren't buried in this village though, but at Verrall; she had been a Verrall by birth —perhaps that's why they came to this neighborhood —it was the name of a great family in those days, you know. . . . There was another woman in the old story, as it went, and she got hold of Mr. Carwithen and was for making him put his wife aside; and so, perhaps, he would have done, but the poor lady died suddenly, and there was some talk about it, having the other woman in the house at the time, and it being so convenient for

both of them. . . . But he didn't marry the other
woman, because he died six months after his wife. . . .
By his will he left all his wife's money to found these
almshouses.

"Dr. Dilke asked if he could see the house where the
Carwithens had lived.

"'It belongs to a London gentleman,' the old man
said, 'who never comes here. It's going to be pulled
down and the land sold in building lots; why, it's been
locked up these ten years or more. I don't suppose it's
been inhabited since—no, not for a hundred years.'

"'Well, I'm looking for a house round about here. I
don't mind spending a little money on repairs if that
house is in the market.'

"The old man didn't know whether it was in the
market or not, but kept repeating that the property was
to be sold and broken up for building lots.

"I won't bother you with all our delays and argu-
ments, but merely tell you that we did finally discover
the lodgekeeper of the estate, who gave us the key. It
was not such a very large estate, nothing to be com-
pared to Verrall, but had been, in its time, of some pre-
tension. Builders' boards had already been raised along
the high road frontage. There were some fine old trees,
black and bare, in a little park. As we turned in
through the rusty gates and motored toward the house
it was nearly dark, but we had our electric torches and
the powerful head lamps of the car. Dr. Dilke made no
comment on what we had found, but he reconstructed
the story of the Carwithens whose names were on that
black stone in Verrall church.

"'They were quarreling over money, he was trying to

get her to sign a will in his favor; she had some little sickness perhaps—brought on probably by rage—he had got the other woman in the house, remember; I expect he was no good. There was some sort of poison about—perhaps for a face wash, perhaps as a drug. He put it in the milk and gave it to her.'

"Here I interrupted: 'How do you know it was in the milk?'

"The doctor did not reply to this. I had now swung the car round to the front of the ancient mansion—a poor, pretentious place, sinister in the half-darkness.

"'And then, when he had done it,' continued Dr. Dilke, mounting the steps of the house, 'he repented most horribly; he wanted to fly for a doctor to get some antidote for the poison with the idea in his head that if he could have got help he could have saved her himself. The other woman kept on laughing. He couldn't forgive her that—that she could laugh at a moment like that; he couldn't get help! He couldn't find a doctor. His wife died. No one suspected foul play—they seldom did in those days as long as the people were respectable; you must remember the state in which medical knowledge was in 1830. He couldn't marry the other woman, and he couldn't touch the money; he left it all to found the almshouses; then he died himself, six months afterward, leaving instructions that his name should be added to that black stone. I dare say he died by his own hand. Probably he loved her through it all, you know—it was only the money, that cursed money, a fortune just within his grasp, but which he couldn't take.'

"'A pretty romance,' I suggested, as we entered the

house; 'I am sure there is a three-volume novel in it of what Mrs. Janey would call "the good old-fashioned" sort.'

"To this Dr. Dilke answered: 'Suppose the miserable man can't rest? Supposing he is still searching for a doctor?'

"We passed from one room to another of the dismal, dusty, dismantled house. Dr. Dilke opened a damaged shutter which concealed one of the windows at the back, and pointed out in the waning light a decayed garden with stone steps and a fishpond; and a low gateway to pass through which a man of his height would have had to stoop. We could just discern this in the twilight. He made no comment. We went upstairs."

Here Cuming paused dramatically to give us the full flavor of the final part of his story. He reminded us, rather unnecessarily, for somehow he had convinced us that this was all perfectly true.

"I am not romancing; I won't answer for what Dr. Dilke said or did, or his adventure of the night before, or the story of the Carwithens as he constructed it, but *this* is actually what happened. . . . We went upstairs by the wide main stairs. Dr. Dilke searched about for and found a door which opened on to the back stairs, and then he said: 'This must be the room.' It was entirely devoid of any furniture, and stained with damp, the walls stripped of paneling and cheaply covered with decayed paper, peeling, and in parts fallen.

"'What's this?' said Dr. Dilke.

"He picked up a scrap of paper that showed vivid on the dusty floor and handed it to me. It was a prescription. He took out his notebook and showed me the page where this fitted in.

" 'This page I tore out last night when I wrote that prescription in this room. The bed was just there, and there was the table on which were the papers and the glass of milk.'

" 'But you couldn't have been here last night,' I protested feebly, 'the locked doors—the whole thing! . . .'

"Dr. Dilke said nothing. After a while neither did I. 'Let's get out of this place,' I said. Then another thought struck me. 'What is your prescription?' I asked.

"He said: 'A very uncommon kind of prescription, a very desperate sort of prescription, one that I've never written before, nor I hope shall again—an antidote for severe arsenical poisoning.'

"I leave you," smiled Cuming, "to your various attitudes of incredulity or explanation."

On Christmas Day in the Morning

MARGERY ALLINGHAM

"What is it," asked the misanthropic writer Ambrose Bierce in the nineteenth century, "that makes human beings at Christmas request a very carnival of crime?" The mystery story, the ghost story, the supernatural were the best of reading then. It was a question that still could be asked in the twentieth century as some of our most delightful authors, Agatha Christie, Dorothy Sayers, and Margery Allingham, regularly offered their treasure, their gift, their Christmas mystery.

Margery Allingham, who began her writing at the age of seven, was a domesticated person who offered very domesticated Christmas stories. She never belonged, as she said herself, to any rigid school of thought; and she believed the only proper study of mankind was man, and the only proper study of woman-kind was woman. So, here is a delightful old woman —one of those charming old ladies that Miss All-

*ingham was able to re-create from first-hand knowl-
edge. Miss Allingham grew up in a small village and
lived most of her life surrounded by horses, dogs, and
gardens in rural Essex.*

Sir Leo Pursuivant, the Chief Constable, had been
sitting in his comfortable study after a magnificent
lunch and talking heavily of the sadness of Christmas,
while his guest, Mr. Campion, most favoured of his
large house-party, had been laughing at him gently.

It was true, the younger man had admitted, his pale
eyes sleepy behind his horn-rimmed spectacles, that,
however good the organization, the festival was never
quite the same after one was six and a half, but then,
what sensible man would expect it to be, and meanwhile, what a truly remarkable bird that had been!

At that point the Superintendent had arrived with
his grim little story and the atmosphere was spoiled altogether.

The policeman sat in a highbacked chair, against a
panelled wall festooned with holly and tinsel, his round
black eyes hard and preoccupied under his short grey
hair. Superintendent Pussey was one of those lean and
urgent countrymen who never quite lose their innate
fondness for a wonder. Despite years of experience the
thing that simply could not have happened and yet in-
dubitably *had* retained a place in his cosmos. He was
holding forth about the latest example. It had already
ruined his Christmas and had kept a great many other
people out in the sleet all day, but nothing would induce him to leave it alone even for five minutes. A heap

of turkey sandwiches was disappearing as he talked and a glass of scotch and soda stood untasted at his side.

"You can see I had to come at once," he was saying. "I had to. I don't see what happened and that's a fact. It's a sort of miracle. Besides, fancy killing a poor old postman on Christmas morning! That's inhuman isn't it? Unnatural?"

Sir Leo nodded his white head. "Let me get this clear: the dead man appears to have been run down at the Benham cross roads. . . ."

Pussey took a handful of cigarettes from the box at his side and arranged them in a cross on the shining surface of the table.

"Look," he said, "here is the Ashby road with a slight bend in it and here, running at right angles, slap through the curve, is the Benham road. You know as well as I do, sir, they're both good wide main thoroughfares as roads go in these parts. This morning the Benham postman, old Fred Noakes, came along the Benham Road loaded down with mail."

"On a bicycle," murmured Campion.

"Naturally. On a bicycle. He called at the last farm before the cross roads and left just about ten o'clock. We know that because he had a cup of tea there. Then his way led him over the crossing and on towards Benham proper."

He paused and looked up from his cigarettes.

"There was very little traffic early to-day, terrible weather all the time, and quite a bit of activity later, so we've got no skid marks to help us. Well, no one seems to have seen old Noakes until close on half an hour later. Then the Benham constable, who lives some three hundred yards from the crossing, came out of his house and walked down to his gate. He saw the postman at once, lying in the middle of the road across his machine. He was dead then."

"He had been trying to carry on?"

"Yes. He was walking, pushing the bike, and he'd dropped in his tracks. There was a depressed fracture in the side of his skull where something—say a car mirror—had struck him. I've got the doctor's report. Meanwhile there's something else."

He returned to his second line of cigarettes.

"Just about ten o'clock there were a couple of fellows walking here on the *Ashby* road. They report that they were almost run down by a saloon car which came up behind them. It missed them and careered off out of their sight round the bend towards the crossing.

"A few minutes later, half a mile farther on, on the other side of the cross roads, a police car met and succeeded in stopping, the same saloon. There was a row and the driver, getting the wind up suddenly, started up again, skidded and smashed the vehicle on the nearest telephone pole. The car turned out to be stolen and there were four half full bottles of gin in the back. The two occupants were both fighting drunk and are now detained."

Mr. Campion took off his spectacles and blinked at the speaker.

"You suggest that there was a connection, do you? Fred and the gin drinkers met at the cross roads, in fact. Any signs on the car?"

Pussey shrugged his shoulders. "Our chaps are at work on that now. The second smash has complicated things a bit but last time I 'phoned they were hopeful."

"But my dear fellow!" Sir Leo was puzzled. "If you can get expert evidence of a collision between the car and the postman, your worries are over. That is, of course, if the medical evidence permits the theory that the unfortunate fellow picked himself up and struggled the three hundred yards towards the constable's house."

Pussey hesitated.

"There's the trouble," he admitted. "If that was all we'd be sitting pretty, but it's not and I'll tell you why. In that three hundred yards of Benham Road, between the crossing and the spot where old Fred died, there is a stile which leads to a footpath. Down the footpath, the best part of a quarter of a mile away, there is one small cottage and at that cottage letters were delivered this morning. The doctor says Noakes might have staggered the three hundred yards up the road leaning on his bike but he puts his foot down and says the other journey, over the stile, would have been plain impossible. I've talked to him. He's the best man in the world on the job and we shan't shake him on that."

"All of which would argue," observed Mr. Campion brightly, "that the postman met the car after he came back from the cottage—between the stile and the policeman's house."

"That's what the constable thought." Pussey's black eyes were snapping. "As soon as he'd telephoned for help he slipped down to the cottage to see if Noakes had called there. When he found he had, he searched the road. He was mystified though because both he and his missus had been at their window for an hour watching for the mail and they hadn't seen a vehicle of any sort go by either way. If a car did hit the postman where he fell it must have turned and gone back afterwards and that's impossible, for the patrol would have seen it."

Leo frowned at him. "What about the other witnesses? Did they see any second car?"

"No." Pussey's face shone with honest wonder. "I made sure of that. Everybody sticks to it that there was no other car or cart about and a good job too, they say, considering the way the saloon was being driven. As I see it, it's a proper mystery, a kind of not very nice miracle, and those two beauties are going to get away with murder on the strength of it. Whatever our fellows find on the car they'll never get past the doctor's evidence."

Mr. Campion got up sadly. The sleet was beating on the windows and from inside the house came the more cheerful sound of teacups. He nodded to the Chief Constable.

"I fear we shall have to see that footpath before it gets utterly dark, you know," he said. "In this weather conditions may have changed by to-morrow."

Leo sighed.

They stopped their freezing journey at the Benham police station to pick up the constable, who proved to be a pleasant youngster who had known and liked the postman and was anxious to serve as their guide.

They inspected the cross roads and the bend and the

spot where the saloon had come to grief. By the time they reached the stile the world was grey and dismal and all trace of Christmas had vanished.

Mr. Campion climbed over and the others followed him on to the path which was narrow and slippery. It wound out into the mist before them, apparently without end.

The procession slid and scrambled in silence for what seemed a mile only to encounter yet another stile and a plank bridge over a stream leading to a patch of bog. As he struggled out of it Pussey pushed back his dripping hat and gazed at the constable.

"You're not having a game I suppose?" he enquired briefly.

"No, sir, no. The little house is just here. You can't make it out because it's a little bit low. There it is, sir."

He pointed to a hump in the near distance which they had all taken to be a haystack and which now emerged as the roof of a hovel with its back towards them in the wet waste.

"Good Heavens!" Leo regarded its desolation with dismay. "Does anybody actually live here?"

"Oh yes, sir. An old widow lady. Mrs. Fyson's the name."

"Alone? How old?"

"I don't rightly know, sir. Over seventy-five, must be."

Leo grunted and a silence fell on the company. The scene was so forlorn and so unutterably quiet in its loneliness that the world might have died.

Mr. Campion broke the spell.

"This is definitely no walk for a dying man," he said

firmly. "The doctor's evidence is completely convincing, don't you think? Now we're here perhaps we should drop in and see the householder."

"We can't all *get* in," Leo objected. "Perhaps the Superintendent. . . . ?"

"No. You and I will go." Mr. Campion was obstinate, and taking the Chief Constable's arm led him firmly round to the front of the cottage. There was a yellow light in the single window on the ground floor and as they slid up a narrow brick path to a very small door, Leo hung back.

"I hate this," he muttered. "Oh—all right, go on. Knock if you must."

Mr. Campion obeyed, stooping so that his head might miss the lintel. There was a movement inside and, at once, the door was opened very wide so that he was startled by the rush of warmth from within.

A little old woman stood before him, peering up without astonishment. He was principally aware of bright eyes.

"Oh dear," she said unexpectedly. "You *are* damp. Come in." And then, looking past him at the skulking Leo. "Two of you! Well, isn't that nice. Mind your poor heads."

The visit became a social occasion before they were well in the room. Her complete lack of surprise or question coupled with the extreme lowness of the ceiling gave her an advantage from which the interview never entirely recovered.

From the first she did her best to put them at their ease.

"You'll have to sit down at once," she said, waving

them to two chairs, one on either side of the small black kitchener. "Most people have to. I'm all right, you see, because I'm not tall. This is my chair here. You must undo that," she went on touching Leo's coat, "otherwise you may take cold when you go out. It is so very chilly isn't it? But so seasonable and that's always nice."

Afterwards it was Mr. Campion's belief that neither he nor the Chief Constable had a word to say for themselves for the first five minutes. They were certainly seated and looking round the one downstairs room the house contained before anything approaching conversation took place.

It was not a sordid interior yet the walls were discoloured, the furniture old without being in any way antique and the place could hardly have been called neat. But at the moment it was festive. There was holly over the two pictures and on the mantel, above the stove, a crowd of bright Christmas cards.

Their hostess sat between them, near the table. It was set for a small tea party and the oil lamp with the red and white frosted glass shade which stood in the centre of it shed a comfortable light on her serene face.

She was a short plump old person whose white hair was brushed tightly to her little round head. Her clothes were all knitted and of an assortment of colours and with them she wore, most unsuitably, a Maltese silk lace collarette and a heavy gold chain. It was only when they noticed she was blushing that they realized she was shy.

"Oh," she exclaimed at last, making a move which put their dumbness to shame. "I quite forgot to say it before! A Merry Christmas to you. Isn't it wonderful how it keeps coming round? It's such a *happy* time, isn't it?"

Leo took himself in hand.

"I do apologize," he began. "This is an imposition on such a day."

"Not at all," she said. "Visitors are a great treat. Not everybody braves my footpath in the winter."

"But some people do, of course?" ventured Mr. Campion.

"Of course." She shot him her shy smile. "Always once a week. They send down from the village every Friday and only this morning a young man, the policeman to be exact, came all the way over to the fields to wish me the compliments of the season and to know if I'd got my post!"

"And you had!" Leo glanced at the array of cards with relief. He was a kindly, sentimental, family man with a horror of loneliness.

She nodded at the brave collection with deep affection.

"It's lovely to see them all up there again, it's one of the real joys of Christmas, isn't it? Messages from people you love and who love you and all so *pretty*, too."

"Did you come down bright and early to meet the postman?" The Chief Constable's question was disarmingly innocent but she looked ashamed and dropped her eyes.

"I wasn't up! Wasn't it dreadful? I was late this morning. In fact, I was only just picking the letters off the mat there when the policeman called. He helped me gather them, the nice boy. There was such a lot. I lay lazily in bed this morning thinking of them instead of moving."

"Still, you knew they were there."

"Oh yes." She sounded content. "I knew they were there. May I offer you a cup of tea? I'm waiting for my Christmas party to arrive, just a woman and her dear greedy little boy; they won't be long. In fact, when I heard your knock I thought they were here already."

Mr. Campion, who had risen to inspect the display of cards on the mantel shelf more closely, helped her to move the kettle so that it should not boil too soon.

The cards were splendid. There were nearly thirty of them in all, and the envelopes which had contained them were packed in a neat bundle and tucked behind the clock.

In design they were mostly conventional. There were robins and firesides, saints and angels, with a secondary line in pictures of gardens in unseasonable bloom, and Scots terriers in tam o' shanter caps. One magnificent affair was entirely in ivorine with a cut-out disclosing a coach and horses surrounded with roses and forget-me-nots. The written messages were all warm and personal —all breathing affection and friendliness and the out-spoken joy of the season:

"The very best to you Darling from All at the Limes"; "To dear Auntie from Little Phil"; "Love and Memories. Edith and Ted"; "There is no wish like the old wish. Warm regards George"; "For dearest Mother"; "Cheerio. Lots of love. Just off. Writing. Take care of yourself. Sonny"; "For dear little Agnes with love from US ALL."

Mr. Campion stood before them for a long time but at length he turned away. He had to stoop to avoid the beam and yet he towered over the old woman who stood watching him.

Something had happened. It had suddenly become very still in the house. The gentle hissing of the kettle sounded unnaturally loud. The recollection of their loneliness returned to chill the cosy room.

The old lady had lost her smile and there was wariness in her eyes.

"Tell me," Mr. Campion spoke very gently. "How do you do it? Do you put them all down there on the mat in their envelopes before you go to bed on Christmas Eve?"

While the point of his question was dawning upon Leo, there was complete silence. It was breathless and unbearable until old Mrs. Fyson pierced it with a laugh of genuine naughtiness.

"Well," she said devastatingly, "it does make it more fun, doesn't it?" She glanced back at Leo whose handsome face was growing scarlet.

"Then. . . ." He was having difficulty with his voice.

"Then the postman did *not* call this morning, ma'am?"

"The postman never calls here except when he brings something from the Government," she said pleasantly. "Everybody gets letters from the Government nowadays, don't they? But he doesn't call here with *personal* letters because, you see, I'm the last of us." She paused and frowned very faintly. It rippled like a shadow over the smoothness of her quiet, careless brow. "There's been so many wars," she said.

"But, dear Lady. . . ." Leo was completely overcome.

She patted his arm to comfort him.

"My dear man," she said kindly. "Don't be
distressed. This isn't sad. It's Christmas. They sent me
their love at Christmas and *I've still got it*. At Christmas I remember them and they remember me I expect
—wherever they are." Her eyes strayed to the ivorine
card with the coach on it. "I do sometimes wonder
about poor *George*," she remarked seriously. "He was
my husband's elder brother and he really did have
quite a shocking life. But he sent me that remarkable
card one year and I kept it with the others . . . after
all, we ought to be charitable, oughtn't we? At Christmas."

As the four men plodded back through the fields,
Pussey was jubilant.

"That's done the trick," he said. "Cleared up the
mystery and made it all plain sailing. We'll get those
two crooks for doing in poor old Noakes. The old girl
was just cheering herself up and you fell for it, eh, constable? Oh don't worry, my boy. There's no harm done
and it's a thing that might have deceived anybody. Just
let it be a lesson to you. I know how it happened. You
didn't want to worry the old thing with the tale of a
death on Christmas morning so you took the sight of
the letters as evidence and didn't go into it. As it turned
out, you were wrong. That's life."

He thrust the young man on ahead of him and
waited for Campion.

"What beats me is how you cottoned to it," he confided. "What gave you the idea?"

"I merely read it, I'm afraid," Mr. Campion was apologetic. "All the envelopes were there, sticking out from behind at the postmark. It was 1914."

Pussey laughed. "Given to you!" he chuckled. "Still I bet you had a job to trust your own eyes."

"Ah." Mr. Campion's voice was thoughtful in the dusk. "That, Super, that was the really difficult bit."

Thirteen at Table

LORD DUNSANY

*Why ghost stories at Christmas? Of course there are
ghosts for all times of the year, particularly, for example, at Halloween. But the Christmas ghost or ghosts
are special.*

*There is a long rich traditional history in many coun-
tries of the world about such Christmas spirits. Christmas comes, as did the winter solstice, at the darkest
time of the year. Our ancestors thought in primitive
time that the dead walked in that brooding darkness;
goblins might gather you up and you'd be "taken to the
mountains" for life. Christmas Eve held many such
threats, and the ghosts and goblins were propitiated by
gifts, bribed by food, comforted by hospitality.*

*Lord Dunsany, whose Irish heritage inspired his al-
most mythical love of the land, had an easy familiarity
with spirits of wonder and an easy camaraderie with
ghosts.*

IN FRONT of a spacious fire-place of the old kind, when the logs were well alight, and men with pipes and glasses were gathered before it in great easeful chairs, and the wild weather outside and the comfort that was within, and the season of the year—for it was Christmas—and the hour of the night, all called for the weird or uncanny, then out spoke the ex-master of foxhounds and told this tale.

"I once had an odd experience too. It was when I had the Bromley and Sydenham, the year I gave them up—as a matter of fact it was the last day of the season. It was no use going on because there were no foxes left in the country, and London was sweeping down on us. You could see it from the kennels all along the skyline like a terrible army in grey, and masses of villas every year came skirmishing down our valleys. Our coverts were mostly on the hills, and as the town came down upon the valleys the foxes used to leave them and go right away out of the country, and they never returned. I think they went by night and moved great distances. Well, it was early April and we had drawn blank all day, and at the last draw of all, the very last of the season, we found a fox. He left the covert with his back to London and its railways and villas and wire, and slipped away towards the chalk country and open Kent. I felt as I once felt as a child on one summer's day when I found a door in a garden where I played left luckily ajar, and I pushed it open and the wide lands were before me and waving fields of corn.

"We settled down into a steady gallop and the fields

began to drift by under us, and a great wind arose full
of fresh breath. We left the clay lands where the
bracken grows and came to a valley at the edge of the
chalk. As we went down into it we saw the fox go up
the other side like a shadow that crosses the evening,
and glide into a wood that stood on the top. We saw a
flash of primroses in the wood and we were out the
other side, hounds hunting perfectly and the fox still
going absolutely straight. It began to dawn on me then
that we were in for a great hunt; I took a deep breath
when I thought of it; the taste of the air of that perfect
spring afternoon as it came to one galloping, and the
thought of a great run, were together like some old rare
wine. Our faces now were to another valley, large fields
led down to it with easy hedges, at the bottom of it a
bright blue stream went singing and a rambling village
smoked, the sunlight on the opposite slopes danced like
a fairy; and all along the top old woods were frowning,
but they dreamed of spring. The fields had fallen off
and were far behind and my only human companion
was James, my old first whip, who had a hound's instinct, and a personal animosity against a fox that even
embittered his speech.

"Across the valley the fox went as straight as a railway line, and again we went without a check straight
through the woods at the top. I remember hearing men
sing or shout as they walked home from work, and
sometimes children whistled; the sounds came up from
the village to the woods at the top of the valley. After
that we saw no more villages, but valley after valley
arose and fell before us as though we were voyaging
some strange and stormy sea; and all the way before us

the fox went dead up-wind like the fabulous flying Dutchman. There was no one in sight now but my first whip and me; we had both of us got on to our second horses as we drew the last covert. Two or three times we checked in those great lonely valleys beyond the village, but I began to have inspirations; I felt a strange certainty within me that this fox was going on straight up-wind till he died or until night came and we could hunt no longer, so I reversed ordinary methods and only cast straight ahead, and always we picked up the scent again at once. I believe that this fox was the last one left in the villa-haunted lands and that he was prepared to leave them for remote uplands far from men, that if we had come the following day he would not have been there, and that we just happened to hit off his journey.

"Evening began to descend upon the valleys, still the hounds drifted on, like the lazy but unresting shadows of clouds upon a summer's day; we heard a shepherd calling to his dog, we saw two maidens move toward a hidden farm, one of them singing softly; no other sounds but ours disturbed the leisure and the loneliness of haunts that seemed not yet to have known the inventions of steam and gunpowder.

"And now the day and our horses were wearing out, but that resolute fox held on. I began to work out the run and to wonder where we were. The last landmark I had ever seen before must have been over five miles back, and from there to the start was at least ten miles more. If only we could kill! Then the sun set. I wondered what chance we had of killing our fox. I looked at James' face as he rode beside me. He did not seem to have lost any confidence, yet his horse was as tired as mine. It was a good clear twilight and the scent was as strong as ever, and the fences were easy enough, but those valleys were terribly trying, and they still rolled on and on. It looked as if the light would outlast all possible endurance both of the fox and the horses, if the scent held good and he did not go to ground, otherwise night would end it. For long we had seen no houses and no roads, only chalk slopes with the twilight on them, and here and there some sheep, and scattered copses darkening in the evening. At some moment I seemed to realize all at once that the light was spent and that darkness was hovering. I looked at James, he was solemnly shaking his head. Suddenly in a little wooded valley we saw climb over the oaks the red-brown gables of a queer old house; at that instant I saw the fox scarcely leading by fifty yards. We blundered through a wood into full sight of the house, but no avenue led up to it or even a path, nor were there any signs of wheel-marks anywhere. Already lights shone here and there in windows. We were in a park, and a fine park, but unkempt beyond credibility; brambles grew every-where. It was too dark to see the fox any more, but we knew he was dead-beat, the hounds were just before us —and a four-foot railing of oak. I shouldn't have tried it on a fresh horse at the beginning of a run, and here was a horse near his last gasp, but what a run! an event standing out in a life-time, and the hounds, close up on their fox, slipping into the darkness as I hesitated. I de-cided to try it. My horse rose about eight inches and took it fair with his breast, and the oak log flew into handfuls of wet decay,—it was rotten with years. And then we were on a lawn, and at the far end of it the hounds were tumbling over their fox. Fox, horses, and light were all done together at the end of a twenty-mile point. We made some noise then, but nobody came out of the queer old house.

"I felt pretty stiff as I walked round to the hall door with the mask and the brush, while James went with the hounds and the two horses to look for the stables. I rang a bell marvellously encrusted with rust, and after a long while the door opened a little way, revealing a hall with much old armour in it and the shabbiest butler that I have ever known.

"I asked him who lived there. Sir Richard Arlen. I explained that my horse could go no further that night, and that I wished to ask Sir Richard Arlen for a bed.

"'O, no one ever comes here, sir,' said the butler.

"I pointed out that I had come.

"'I don't think it would be possible, sir,' he said.

"This annoyed me, and I asked to see Sir Richard, and insisted until he came. Then I apologized and explained the situation. He looked only fifty, but a 'Varsity oar on the wall with the date of the early seventies made him older than that; his face had something of the shy look of the hermit; he regretted that he had no room to put me up. I was sure that this was untrue, also I had to be put up there, there was nowhere else within miles, so I almost insisted. Then, to my astonishment, he turned to the butler and they talked it over in an undertone. At last they seemed to think that they could manage it, though clearly with reluctance. It was by now seven o'clock, and Sir Richard told me he dined at half-past seven. There was no question of clothes for

me other than those I stood in, as my host was shorter
and broader. He showed me presently to the drawing-
room, and then he reappeared before half-past seven in
evening dress and a white waistcoat. The drawing-
room was large and contained old furniture, but it was
rather worn than venerable; an aubusson carpet
flapped about the floor, the wind seemed momently to
enter the room, and old draughts haunted corners;
stealthy feet of rats that were never at rest indicated
the extent of the ruin that time had wrought in the
wainscot, somewhere far off a shutter flapped to and
fro, the guttering candles were insufficient to light so
large a room. The gloom that these things suggested
was quite in keeping with Sir Richard's first remark to
me after he entered the room.

"'I must tell you, sir, that I have led a wicked life.
O, a very wicked life.'

"Such confidences from a man much older than one-
self after one has known him for half an hour are so
rare that any possible answer merely does not suggest
itself. I said rather slowly, 'O, really,' and chiefly to
forestall another such remark, I said, 'What a charming house you have.'

"'Yes,' he said, 'I have not left it for nearly forty
years. Since I left the 'Varsity. One is young there, you
know, and one has opportunities; but I make no excuses, no excuses.' And the door slipping its rusty latch,
came drifting on the draught into the room, and the
long carpet flapped and the hangings upon the walls,
then the draught fell rustling away and the door
slammed to again.

"'Ah, Marianne,' he said. 'We have a guest to-night.

Mr. Linton. This is Marianne Gib.' And everything became clear to me. 'Mad,' I said to myself, for no one had entered the room.

"The rats ran up the length of the room behind the wainscot ceaselessly, and the wind unlatched the door again and the folds of the carpet fluttered up to our feet and stopped there, for our weight held it down.

" 'Let me introduce Mr. Linton,' said my host. 'Lady Mary Errinjer.'

"The door slammed back again. I bowed politely. Even had I been invited I should have humoured him, but it was the very least that an uninvited guest could do.

"This kind of thing happened eleven times, the rustling, and the fluttering of the carpet, and the footsteps of the rats, and the restless door, and then the sad voice of my host introducing me to phantoms. Then for some while we waited while I struggled with the situation; conversation flowed slowly. And again the draught came trailing up the room, while the flaring candles filled it with hurrying shadows. 'Ah, late again, Cicely,' said my host in his soft mournful way. 'Always late, Cicely.' Then I went down to dinner with that man and his mind and the twelve phantoms that haunted it. I found a long table with fine old silver on it, and places laid for fourteen. The butler was now in evening dress, there were fewer draughts in the dining-room, the scene was less gloomy there. 'Will you sit next to Rosalind at the other end?' Sir Richard said to me. 'She always takes the head of the table. I wronged her most of all.'

"I said, 'I shall be delighted.'

"I looked at the butler closely; but never did I see by any expression of his face, or by anything that he did, any suggestion that he waited upon less than fourteen people in the complete possession of all their faculties. Perhaps a dish appeared to be refused more often than taken, but every glass was equally filled with champagne. At first I found little to say, but when Sir Richard, speaking from the far end of the table, said, 'You are tired, Mr. Linton?' I was reminded that I owed something to a host upon whom I had forced myself. It was excellent champagne, and with the help of a second glass I made the effort to begin a conversation with a Miss Helen Errold, for whom the place upon one side of me was laid. It came more easy to me very soon; I frequently paused in my monologue, like Mark Antony, for a reply, and sometimes I turned and spoke to Miss Rosalind Smith. Sir Richard at the other end talked sorrowfully on; he spoke as a condemned man might speak to his judge, and yet somewhat as a judge might speak to one that he once condemned wrongly. My own mind began to turn to mournful things. I drank another glass of champagne, but I was still thirsty. I felt as if all the moisture in my body had been blown away over the downs of Kent by the wind up which we had galloped. Still I was not talking enough: my host was looking at me. I made another effort; after all I had something to talk about: a twenty-mile point is not often seen in a lifetime, especially south of the Thames. I began to describe the run to Rosalind Smith. I could see then that my host was pleased, the sad look in his face gave a kind of a flicker, like mist upon the mountains on a miserable day when a faint puff comes from the sea and

the mist would lift if it could. And the butler refilled
my glass very attentively. I asked her first if she hunted,
and paused and began my story. I told her where we
found the fox and how fast and straight he had gone,
and how I had got through the village by keeping to
the road, while the little gardens and wire, and then
the river had stopped the rest of the field. I told her the
kind of country that we crossed and how splendid it
looked in the spring, and how mysterious the valleys
were as soon as the twilight came, and what a glorious
horse I had and how wonderfully he went.

"I was so fearfully thirsty after the great hunt that I
had to stop for a moment now and then, but I went on
with my description of that famous run, for I had
warmed to the subject, and after all there was nobody
to tell of it but me except my old whipper-in, and 'the
old fellow's probably drunk by now' I thought. I described to her minutely the exact spot in the run at
which it had come to me clearly that this was going to
be the greatest hunt in the whole history of Kent.
Sometimes I forgot incidents that had happened, as
one well may in a run of twenty miles, and then I had
to fill in the gaps by inventing. I was pleased to be able
to make the party go off well by means of my conversation, and besides that the lady to whom I was speaking was extremely pretty: I do not mean in a flesh-and-
blood kind of way, but there were little shadowy lines
about the chair beside me that hinted at an unusually
graceful figure when Miss Rosalind Smith was alive;
and I began to perceive that what I first mistook for
the smoke of guttering candles and a tablecloth waving
in the draught was in reality an extremely animated

company who listened, and not without interest, to my story of by far the greatest hunt that the world had ever known: indeed, I told them that I would confidently go further and predict that never in the history of the world would there be such a run again. Only my throat was terribly dry.

"And then, as it seemed, they wanted to hear more about my horse. I had forgotten that I had come there on a horse, but when they reminded me it all came back; they looked so charming leaning over the table, intent upon what I said, that I told them everything they wanted to know. Everything was going so pleasantly if only Sir Richard would cheer up. I heard his mournful voice every now and then—these were very pleasant people if only he would take them the right way. I could understand that he regretted his past, but the early seventies seemed centuries away, and I felt now that he misunderstood these ladies, they were not revengeful as he seemed to suppose. I wanted to show him how cheerful they really were, and so I made a joke and they all laughed at it, and then I chaffed them a bit, especially Rosalind, and nobody resented it in the very least. And still Sir Richard sat there with that unhappy look, like one that has ended weeping because it is vain and has not the consolation even of tears.

"We had been a long time there, and many of the candles had burnt out, but there was light enough. I was glad to have an audience for my exploit, and being happy myself I was determined Sir Richard should be. I made more jokes and they still laughed good-naturedly; some of the jokes were a little broad perhaps, but no harm was meant. And then,—I do not wish to excuse myself, but I had had a harder day than I ever had had before, and without knowing it I must have been completely exhausted; in this state the champagne had found me, and what would have been harmless at any other time must somehow have got the better of me when quite tired out. Anyhow, I went too far, I made some joke,—I cannot in the least remember what—that suddenly seemed to offend them. I felt all at once a commotion in the air; I looked up and saw that they had all risen from the table and were sweeping towards the door. I had not time to open it, but it blew open on a wind; I could scarcely see what Sir Richard was doing because only two candles were left, I think the rest blew out when the ladies suddenly rose. I sprang up to apologize, to assure them—and then fatigue overcame me as it had overcome my horse at the last fence, I clutched at the table, but the cloth came away, and then I fell. The fall, and the darkness on the floor, and the pent-up fatigue of the day overcame me all three together.

"The sun shone over glittering fields and in at a bedroom window, and thousands of birds were chaunting to the spring, and there I was in an old four-poster bed in a quaint old panelled bedroom, fully dressed, and wearing long muddy boots; someone had taken my spurs and that was all. For a moment I failed to realize, and then it all came back—my enormity and the pressing need of an abject apology to Sir Richard. I pulled an embroidered bell-rope until the butler came; he came in perfectly cheerful and indescribably shabby. I asked him if Sir Richard was up, and he said he had just gone down, and told me to my amazement that it was twelve o'clock. I asked to be shown in to Sir Richard at once.

"He was in his smoking-room. 'Good morning,' he said cheerfully the moment I went in. I went directly to the matter in hand. 'I fear that I insulted some ladies in your house . . .' I began.

" 'You did indeed,' he said. 'You did indeed.' And then he burst into tears, and took me by the hand. 'How can I ever thank you?' he said to me then. 'We have been thirteen at table for thirty years, and I never dared to insult them because I had wronged them all, and now you have done it, and I know they will never dine here again.' And for a long time he still held my hand, and then he gave it a grip and a kind of a shake which I took to mean 'good-bye,' and I drew my hand away then and left the house. And I found James in the disused stables with the hounds and asked him how he had fared, and James, who is a man of very few words, said he could not rightly remember, and I got my spurs from the butler and climbed on to my horse; and slowly we rode away from that queer old house, and slowly we wended home, for the hounds were foot-sore but happy and the horses were tired still. And when we recalled that the hunting season was ended, we turned our faces to spring and thought of the new things that try to replace the old. And that very year I heard, and have often heard since, of dances and happier dinners at Sir Richard Arlen's house."

Wolverden Tower

GRANT ALLEN

*Come gather around now for a Christmas Gothic. In-
deed, is not Christmas the most Gothic time of all? The
black trees look like old castle battlements against the
snow. This is a time when the simplest of homes becomes a fortress. Now is the time when the smallest of
fires kindles the imagination.*

*Grant Allen, a contemporary of Sir Arthur Conan
Doyle, was also fortunate to have the creator of Sherlock Holmes as a neighbor. Both took particular pleasure in Christmas. "Wolverden Tower," by Grant Allen
was one of Doyle's favorite tales.*

*This fascinating and forgotten foray into the super-
natural has a flavor of the true Christmas past. It is the
Christmas that still lingered in parts of Britain—a
Christmas that had been imported in the days of the
Vikings, whose feast of Jul, our Yule time, was in honor
of the god Thor. "Welcome Yule," we say, little realizing what ancient time that expression conjures up.*

MAISIE LLEWELYN had never been asked to Wolverden before; therefore, she was not a little elated at Mrs. West's invitation. For Wolverden Hall, one of the loveliest Elizabethan manor-houses in the Weald of Kent, had been bought and fitted up in appropriate style (the phrase is the upholsterer's) by Colonel West, the famous millionaire from South Australia. The Colonel had lavished upon it untold wealth, fleeced from the backs of ten thousand sheep and an equal number of his fellow-countrymen; and Wolverden was now, if not the most beautiful, at least the most opulent country-house within easy reach of London.

Mrs. West was waiting at the station to meet Maisie. The house was full of Christmas guests already, it is true; but Mrs. West was a model of stately, old-fashioned courtesy: she would not have omitted meeting one among the number on any less excuse than a royal command to appear at Windsor. She kissed Maisie on both cheeks—she had always been fond of Maisie —and, leaving two haughty young aristocrats (in powdered hair and blue-and-gold livery) to hunt up her luggage by the light of nature, sailed forth with her through the door to the obsequious carriage.

The drive up the avenue to Wolverden Hall Maisie found quite delicious. Even in their leafless winter condition the great limes looked so noble; and the ivy-covered hall at the end, with its mullioned windows, its Inigo Jones porch, and its creeper-clad gables, was as picturesque a building as the ideals one sees in Mr. Abbey's sketches. If only Arthur Hume had been one of the party now, Maisie's joy would have been complete. But what was the use of thinking so much about Arthur

Hume, when she didn't even know whether Arthur Hume cared for her?

A tall, slim girl, Maisie Llewelyn, with rich black hair, and ethereal features, as became a descendant of Llewelyn ap Iorwerth—the sort of girl we none of us would have called anything more than 'interesting' till Rossetti and Burne-Jones found eyes for us to see that the type is beautiful with a deeper beauty than that of your obvious pink-and-white prettiness. Her eyes, in particular, had a lustrous depth that was almost super-human, and her fingers and nails were strangely trans-parent in their waxen softness.

"You won't mind my having put you in a ground-floor room in the new wing, my dear, will you?" Mrs. West inquired, as she led Maisie personally to the quar-ters chosen for her. "You see, we're so unusually full, because of these tableaux!"

Maisie gazed round the ground-floor room in the new wing with eyes of mute wonder. If *this* was the kind of lodging for which Mrs. West thought it neces-sary to apologize, Maisie wondered of what sort were those better rooms which she gave to the guests she delighted to honour. It was a large and exquisitely dec-orated chamber, with the softest and deepest Oriental carpet Maisie's feet had ever felt, and the daintiest cur-tains her eyes had ever lighted upon. True, it opened by french windows on to what was nominally the ground in front; but as the Italian terrace, with its formal balustrade and its great stone balls, was raised several feet above the level of the sloping garden below, the room was really on the first floor for all practical pur-poses. Indeed, Maisie rather liked the unwonted sense of space and freedom which was given by this easy access to the world without; and, as the windows were secured by great shutters and fasteners, she had no counterbalancing fear lest a nightly burglar should attempt to carry off her little pearl necklet or her amethyst brooch, instead of directing his whole attention to Mrs. West's famous diamond tiara.

She moved naturally to the window. She was fond of nature. The view it disclosed over the Weald at her feet was wide and varied. Misty range lay behind misty range, in a faint December haze, receding and receding, till away to the south, half hidden by vapour, the Sussex downs loomed vague in the distance. The village church, as happens so often in the case of old lordly manors, stood within the grounds of the Hall, and close by the house. It had been built, her hostess said, in the days of the Edwards, but had portions of an older Saxon edifice still enclosed in the chancel. The one eyesore in the view was its new white tower, recently restored (or rather, rebuilt), which contrasted most painfully with the mellow grey stone and mouldering corbels of the nave and transept.

"What a pity it's been so spoiled!" Maisie exclaimed, looking across at the tower. Coming straight as she did from a Merioneth rectory, she took an ancestral interest in all that concerned churches.

"Oh, my dear!" Mrs. West cried, *"please* don't say that, I beg of you, to the Colonel. If you were to murmur "spoiled" to him you'd wreck his digestion. He's spent ever so much money over securing the foundations and reproducing the sculpture on the old tower

we took down, and it breaks his dear heart when anybody disapproves of it. For *some* people, you know, are
so absurdly opposed to reasonable restoration."

"Oh, but this isn't even restoration, you know,"
Maisie said, with the frankness of twenty, and the spe-
cialist interest of an antiquary's daughter. "This is pure
reconstruction."

"Perhaps so," Mrs. West answered. "But if you think
so, my dear, don't breathe it at Wolverden."

A fire, of ostentatiously wealthy dimensions, and of
the best glowing coal, burned bright on the hearth; but
the day was mild, and hardly more than autumnal.
Maisie found the room quite unpleasantly hot. She
opened the windows and stepped out on the terrace.
Mrs. West followed her. They paced up and down the
broad gravelled platform for a while—Maisie had not
yet taken off her travelling-cloak and hat—and then
strolled half unconsciously towards the gate of the
church. The churchyard, to hide the tombstones of
which the parapet had been erected, was full of quaint
old monuments, with broken-nosed cherubs, some of
them dating from a comparatively early period. The
porch, with its sculptured niches deprived of their
saints by puritan hands, was still rich and beautiful in
its carved detail. On the seat inside an old woman was
sitting. She did not rise as the lady of the manor
approached, but went on mumbling and muttering in-
articulately to herself in a sulky undertone. Still, Maisie
was aware, none the less, that the moment she came
near a strange light gleamed suddenly in the old
woman's eyes, and that her glance was fixed upon her.

A faint thrill of recognition seemed to pass like a flash through her palsied body. Maisie knew not why, but she was dimly afraid of the old woman's gaze upon her.

"It's a lovely old church!" Maisie said, looking up at the trefoil finials on the porch—"all, except the tower."

"We *had* to reconstruct it," Mrs. West answered apologetically—Mrs. West's general attitude in life was apologetic, as though she felt she had no right to so much more money than her fellow-creatures. "It would have fallen if we hadn't done something to buttress it up. It was really in a most dangerous and critical condition."

"Lies! lies! lies!" the old woman burst out suddenly, though in a strange, low tone, as if speaking to herself. "It would *not* have fallen—they knew it would not. It could not have fallen. It would never have fallen if they had not destroyed it. And even then—I was there when they pulled it down—each stone clung to each, with arms and legs and hands and claws, till they burst them asunder by main force with their new-fangled stuff—I don't know what they call it—dynamite, or something. It was all of it done for one man's vainglory!"

"Come away, dear," Mrs. West whispered. But Maisie loitered.

"Wolverden Tower was fasted thrice," the old woman continued, in a sing-song quaver. "It was fasted thrice with souls of maids against every assault of man or devil. It was fasted at the foundation against earthquake and ruin. It was fasted at the top against thunder and lightning. It was fasted in the middle against storm and battle. And there it would have stood for a thou-

sand years if a wicked man had not raised a vainglo-
rious hand against it. For that's what the rhyme says—

> "Fasted thrice with souls of men,
> Stands the tower of Wolverden;
> Fasted thrice with maidens' blood,
> A thousand years of fire and flood
> Shall see it stand as erst it stood."

She paused a moment, then, raising one skinny hand
towards the brand-new stone, she went on in the same
voice, but with malignant fervour—

> "A thousand years the tower shall stand
> Till ill assailed by evil hand;
> By evil hand in evil hour,
> Fasted thrice with warlock's power,
> Shall fall the stanes of Wulfhere's tower."

She tottered off as she ended, and took her seat on
the edge of a depressed vault in the churchyard close
by, still eyeing Maisie Llewelyn with a weird and curious glance, almost like the look which a famishing man
casts upon the food in a shop-window.

"Who is she?" Maisie asked, shrinking away in
undefined terror.

"Oh, old Bessie," Mrs. West answered, looking more
apologetic (for the parish) than ever. "She's always
hanging about here. She has nothing else to do, and
she's an outdoor pauper. You see, that's the worst of
having the church in one's grounds, which is otherwise
picturesque and romantic and baronial; the road to it is
public; you must admit all the world; and old Bessie

will come here. The servants are afraid of her. They say she's a witch. She has the evil eye, and she drives girls to suicide. But they cross her hand with silver all the same, and she tells them their fortunes—gives them each a butler. She's full of dreadful stories about Wolverden Church—stories to make your blood run cold, my dear, compact with old superstitions and murders, and so forth. And they're true, too, that's the worst of them. She's quite a character. Mr. Blaydes, the antiquary, is really attached to her; he says she's now the sole living repository of the traditional folklore and history of the parish. But I don't care for it myself. It "gars one greet," as we say in Scotland. Too much burying alive in it, don't you know, my dear, to quite suit *my* fancy."

They turned back as she spoke towards the carved wooden lych-gate, one of the oldest and most exquisite of its class in England. When they reached the vault by whose doors old Bessie was seated, Maisie turned once more to gaze at the pointed lancet windows of the Early English choir, and the still more ancient dogtooth ornament of the ruined Norman Lady Chapel.

"How solidly it's built!" she exclaimed, looking up at the arches which alone survived the fury of the Puritan. "It really looks as if it would last for ever."

Old Bessie had bent her head, and seemed to be whispering something at the door of the vault. But at the sound she raised her eyes, and, turning her wizened face towards the lady of the manor, mumbled through her few remaining fang-like teeth an old local saying, "Bradbury for length, Wolverden for strength, and Church Hatton for beauty!

"Three brothers builded churches three;
And fasted thrice each church shall be:
Fasted thrice with maidens' blood,
To make them safe from fire and flood;
Fasted thrice with souls of men,
Hatton, Bradbury, Wolverden!"

"Come away," Maisie said, shuddering. "I'm afraid of that woman. Why was she whispering at the doors of the vault down there? I don't like the look of her."

"My dear," Mrs. West answered, in no less terrified a tone, "I will confess I don't like the look of her myself. I wish she'd leave the place. I've tried to make her. The Colonel offered her fifty pounds down and a nice cottage in Surrey if only she'd go—she frightens me so much; but she wouldn't hear of it. She said she must stop by the bodies of her dead—that's her style, don't you see: a sort of modern ghoul, a degenerate vampire —and from the bodies of her dead in Wolverden Church no living soul should ever move her."

II

For dinner Maisie wore her white satin Empire dress, high-waisted, low-necked, and cut in the bodice with a certain baby-like simplicity of style which exactly suited her strange and uncanny type of beauty. She was very much admired.

After dinner, the tableaux. They had been designed and managed by a famous Royal Academician, and were mostly got up by the members of the house-party.

The first tableau, Maisie learned from the gorgeous programme, was "Jephthah's Daughter." The subject

was represented at the pathetic moment when the
doomed virgin goes forth from her father's house with
her attendant maidens to bewail her virginity for two
months upon the mountains, before the fulfilment of
the awful vow which bound her father to offer her up
for a burnt offering. Maisie thought it too solemn and
tragic a scene for a festive occasion. But the famous
R.A. had a taste for such themes, and his grouping was
certainly most effectively dramatic.

"A perfect symphony in white and grey," said Mr.
Wills, the art critic.

"How awfully affecting!" said most of the young
girls.

"Reminds me a little too much, my dear, of old Bessie's stories," Mrs. West whispered low, leaning from
her seat across two rows to Maisie.

A piano stood a little on one side of the platform,
just in front of the curtain. The intervals between the
pieces were filled up with songs, which, however, had
been evidently arranged in keeping with the solemn
and half-mystical tone of the tableaux. It is the habit of
amateurs to take a long time in getting their scenes in
order, so the interposition of the music was a happy
thought as far as its prime intention went. But Maisie
wondered they could not have chosen some livelier song
for Christmas Eve than "Oh, Mary, go and call the
cattle home, and call the cattle home, and call the cattle home, across the sands of Dee." Her own name was
Mary when she signed it officially, and the sad lilt of
the last line, "But never home came she," rang unpleasantly in her ear through the rest of the evening.

The second tableau was the "Sacrifice of Iphigenia."

It was admirably rendered. The cold and dignified father, standing, apparently unmoved, by the pyre; the
cruel faces of the attendant priests; the shrinking form
of the immolated princess; the mere blank curiosity
and inquiring interest of the helmeted heroes looking
on, to whom this slaughter of a virgin victim was but
an ordinary incident of the Achaean religion—all these
had been arranged by the Academical director with
consummate skill and pictorial cleverness. But the
group that attracted Maisie most among the compo-
nents of the scene was that of the attendant maidens,
more conspicuous here in their flowing white chitons
than even they had been when posed as companions of
the beautiful and ill-fated Hebrew victim. Two in particular excited her close attention—two very graceful
and spiritual-looking girls, in long white robes of no
particular age or country, who stood at the very end
near the right edge of the picture. "How lovely they
are, the two last on the right!" Maisie whispered to her
neighbour—an Oxford undergraduate with a budding
moustache. "I do so admire them!"

"Do you?" he answered, fondling the moustache
with one dubious finger. "Well, now, do you know, I
don't think I do. They're rather coarse-looking. And
besides, I don't quite like the way they've got their hair
done up in bunches; too fashionable, isn't it?—too
much of the present day? I don't care to see a girl in a
Greek costume, with her coiffure so evidently turned
out by Truefitt's!"

"Oh, I don't mean those two," Maisie answered, a
little shocked he should think she had picked out such
meretricious faces; "I mean the two beyond them again

—the two with their hair so simply and sweetly done—
the ethereal-looking dark girls."

The undergraduate opened his mouth, and stared at
her in blank amazement for a moment. "Well, I don't
see—" he began, and broke off suddenly. Something in
Maisie's eye seemed to give him pause. He fondled his
moustache, hesitated, and was silent.

At the end of the tableau one or two of the characters who were not needed in succeeding pieces came
down from the stage and joined the body of spectators,
as they often do, in their character-dresses—a good opportunity, in point of fact, for retaining through the
evening the advantages conferred by theatrical costume, rouge, and pearl-powder. Among them the two
girls Maisie had admired so much glided quietly towards her and took the two vacant seats on either side,
one of which had just been quitted by the awkward undergraduate. They were not only beautiful in face and
figure, on a closer view, but Maisie found them from
the first extremely sympathetic. They burst into talk
with her, frankly and at once, with charming ease and
grace of manner. They were ladies in the grain, in instinct and breeding. The taller of the two, whom the
other addressed as Yolande, seemed particularly pleas-
ing. The very name charmed Maisie. She was friends
with them at once. They both possessed a certain
nameless attraction that constitutes in itself the best
possible introduction. Maisie hesitated to ask them
whence they came, but it was clear from their talk they
knew Wolverden intimately.

After a minute the piano struck up once more. As
chance would have it, the vocalist began singing the

song Maisie most of all hated. It was Scott's ballad of
"Proud Maisie," set to music by Carlo Ludovici—

> "Proud Maisie is in the wood,
>   Walking so early;
> Sweet Robin sits on the bush,
>   Singing so rarely.
>
> 'Tell me, thou bonny bird,
>   When shall I marry me?'
> 'When six braw gentlemen
>   Kirkward shall carry ye.'
>
> 'Who makes the bridal bed,
>   Birdie, say truly?'
> 'The grey-headed sexton
>   That delves the grave duly.
>
> 'The glow-worm o'er grave and stone
>   Shall light thee steady;
> The owl from the steeple sing,
>   "Welcome, proud lady."'"

Maisie listened to the song with grave discomfort.
She had never liked it, and tonight it appalled her. She
did not know that just at that moment Mrs. West was
whispering in a perfect fever of apology to a lady by
her side, "Oh dear! oh dear! what a dreadful thing of
me ever to have permitted that song to be sung here to-
night! It was horribly thoughtless! Why, now I remember, Miss Llewelyn's name, you know, is Maisie!—
and there she is listening to it with a face like a sheet! I
shall never forgive myself!"

The tall, dark girl by Maisie's side, whom the other
called Yolande, leaned across to her sympathetically.

"You don't like that song?" she said, with just a tinge of reproach in her voice as she said it.

"I hate it!" Maisie answered, trying hard to compose herself.

"Why so?" the tall, dark girl asked, in a tone of calm and singular sweetness. "It is sad, perhaps; but it's lovely—and natural!"

"My own name is Maisie," her new friend replied, with an ill-repressed shudder. "And somehow that song pursues me through life. I seem always to hear the horrid ring of the words, 'When six braw gentlemen kirkward shall carry ye.' I wish to heaven my people had never called me Maisie!"

"And yet *why?*" the tall, dark girl asked again, with a sad, mysterious air. "Why this clinging to life—this terror of death—this inexplicable attachment to a world of misery? And with such eyes as yours, too! Your eyes are like mine"—which was a compliment, certainly, for the dark girl's own pair were strangely deep and lustrous. "People with eyes such as those, that can look into futurity, ought not surely to shrink from a mere gate like death! For death is but a gate—the gate of life in its fullest beauty. It is written over the door, '*Mors janua vitae.*'"

"What door?" Maisie asked—for she remembered having read those selfsame words, and tried in vain to translate them, that very day, though the meaning was now clear to her.

The answer electrified her: "The gate of the vault in Wolverden churchyard."

She said it very low, but with pregnant expression.

"Oh, how dreadful!" Maisie exclaimed, drawing back. The tall, dark girl half frightened her.

"Not at all," the girl answered. "This life is so short, so vain, so transitory! And beyond it is peace—eternal peace—the calm of rest—the joy of the spirit."

"You come to anchor at last," her companion added.

"But if—one has somebody one would not wish to leave behind?" Maisie suggested timidly.

"He will follow before long," the dark girl replied with quiet decision, interpreting rightly the sex of the indefinite substantive. "Time passes so quickly. And if time passes quickly in time, how much more, then, in eternity!"

"Hush, Yolande," the other dark girl put in, with a warning glance; "there's a new tableau coming. Let me see, is this 'The Death of Ophelia?' No. That's number four; this is number three, 'The Martyrdom of St. Agnes'."

III

"My dear," Mrs. West said, positively oozing apology, when she met Maisie in the supper-room, "I'm afraid you've been left in a corner by yourself almost all the evening!"

"Oh dear, no," Maisie answered with a quiet smile. "I had that Oxford undergraduate at my elbow at first; and afterwards those two nice girls, with the flowing white dresses and the beautiful eyes, came and sat beside me. What's their name, I wonder?"

"Which girls?" Mrs. West asked, with a little surprise in her tone, for her impression was rather that

Maisie had been sitting between two empty chairs for
the greater part of the evening, muttering at times to
herself in the most uncanny way, but not talking to
anybody.

Maisie glanced round the room in search of her new
friends, and for some time could not see them. At last,
she observed them in a remote alcove, drinking red
wine by themselves out of Venetian-glass beakers.
"Those two," she said, pointing towards them.
"They're such charming girls! Can you tell me who
they are? I've quite taken a fancy to them."

Mrs. West gazed at them for a second—or rather, at
the recess towards which Maisie pointed—and then
turned to Maisie with much the same oddly embar-
rassed look and manner as the undergraduate's. "Oh,
those!" she said slowly, peering through and through
her, Maisie thought. "Those—must be some of the professionals from London. At any rate—I'm not sure
which you mean—over there by the curtain, in the
Moorish nook, you say—well, I can't tell you their
names! So they *must* be professionals."

She went off with a singularly frightened manner.
Maisie noticed it and wondered at it. But it made no
great or lasting impression.

When the party broke up, about midnight or a little
later, Maisie went along the corridor to her own bedroom. At the end, by the door, the two other girls happened to be standing, apparently gossiping.

"Oh, you've not gone home yet?" Maisie said, as she
passed, to Yolande.

"No, we're stopping here," the dark girl with the
speaking eyes answered.

Maisie paused for a second. Then an impulse burst over her. "Will you come and see my room?" she asked, a little timidly.

"Shall we go, Hedda?" Yolande said, with an inquiring glance at her companion.

Her friend nodded assent. Maisie opened the door, and ushered them into her bedroom.

The ostentatiously opulent fire was still burning brightly, the electric light flooded the room with its brilliancy, the curtains were drawn, and the shutters fastened. For a while the three girls sat together by the hearth and gossiped quietly. Maisie liked her new friends—their voices were so gentle, soft, and sympathetic, while for face and figure they might have sat as models to Burne-Jones or Botticelli. Their dresses, too, took her delicate Welsh fancy; they were so dainty, yet so simple. The soft silk fell in natural folds and dimples. The only ornaments they wore were two curious brooches of very antique workmanship—as Maisie supposed—somewhat Celtic in design, and enamelled in blood-red on a gold background. Each carried a flower laid loosely in her bosom. Yolande's was an orchid with long, floating streamers, in colour and shape recalling some Southern lizard; dark purple spots dappled its lip and petals. Hedda's was a flower of a sort Maisie had never before seen—the stem spotted like a viper's skin, green flecked with russet-brown, and uncanny to look upon; on either side, great twisted spirals of red-and-blue blossoms, each curled after the fashion of a scorpion's tail, very strange and lurid. Something weird and witch-like about flowers and dresses rather attracted Maisie; they affected her with the half-repellent fascination of a snake for a bird; she felt such blossoms were fit for incantations and sorceries. But a lily-of-the-valley in Yolande's dark hair gave a sense of purity which assorted better with the girl's exquisitely calm and nun-like beauty.

After a while Hedda rose. "This air is close," she said. "It ought to be warm outside tonight, if one may judge by the sunset. May I open the window?"

"Oh, certainly, if you like," Maisie answered, a vague foreboding now struggling within her against innate politeness.

Hedda drew back the curtains and unfastened the shutters. It was a moonlit evening. The breeze hardly stirred the bare boughs of the silver birches. A sprinkling of soft snow on the terrace and the hills just whitened the ground. The moon lighted it up, falling full upon the Hall; the church and tower below stood silhouetted in dark against a cloudless expanse of starry sky in the background. Hedda opened the window. Cool, fresh air blew in, very soft and genial, in spite of the snow and the lateness of the season. "What a glorious night!" she said, looking up at Orion overhead. "Shall we stroll out for a while in it?"

If the suggestion had not thus been thrust upon her from outside, it would never have occurred to Maisie to walk abroad in a strange place, in evening dress, on a winter's night, with snow whitening the ground; but Hedda's voice sounded so sweetly persuasive, and the idea itself seemed so natural now she had once proposed it, that Maisie followed her two new friends on to the moonlit terrace without a moment's hesitation.

They paced once or twice up and down the gravelled

walks. Strange to say, though a sprinkling of dry snow powdered the ground under foot, the air itself was soft and balmy. Stranger still, Maisie noticed, almost without noticing it, that though they walked three abreast, only one pair of footprints—her own—lay impressed on the snow in a long trail when they turned at either end and re-paced the platform. Yolande and Hedda must step lightly indeed; or perhaps her own feet might be warmer or thinner shod, so as to melt the light layer of snow more readily.

The girls slipped their arms through hers. A little thrill coursed through her. Then, after three or four turns up and down the terrace, Yolande led the way quietly down the broad flight of steps in the direction of the church on the lower level. In that bright, broad moonlight Maisie went with them undeterred; the Hall was still alive with the glare of electric lights in bedroom windows; and the presence of the other girls, both wholly free from any signs of fear, took off all sense of terror or loneliness. They strolled on into the churchyard. Maisie's eyes were now fixed on the new white tower, which merged in the silhouette against the starry sky into much the same grey and indefinite hue as the older parts of the building. Before she quite knew where she was, she found herself at the head of the worn stone steps which led into the vault by whose doors she had seen old Bessie sitting. In the pallid moonlight, with the aid of the greenish reflection from the snow, she could just read the words inscribed over the portal, the words that Yolande had repeated in the drawing room, *"Mors janua vitae."*

Yolande moved down one step. Maisie drew back for

the first time, with a faint access of alarm. "You're—you're not *going down* there!" she exclaimed, catching her breath for a second.

"Yes, I am," her new friend answered in a calmly quiet voice. "Why not? We live here."

"You live here?" Maisie echoed, freeing her arms by a sudden movement and standing away from her mysterious friends with a tremulous shudder.

"Yes, we live here," Hedda broke in, without the slightest emotion. She said it in a voice of perfect calm, as one might say it of any house in a street in London.

Maisie was far less terrified than she might have imagined beforehand would be the case under such unexpected conditions. The two girls were so simple, so natural, so strangely like herself, that she could not say she was really afraid of them. She shrank, it is true, from the nature of the door at which they stood, but she received the unearthly announcement that they lived there with scarcely more than a slight tremor of surprise and astonishment.

"You will come in with us?" Hedda said in a gently enticing tone. "We went into your bedroom."

Maisie hardly liked to say no. They seemed so anxious to show her their home. With trembling feet she moved down the first step, and then the second. Yolande kept ever one pace in front of her. As Maisie reached the third step, the two girls, as if moved by one design, took her wrists in their hands, not unkindly, but coaxingly. They reached the actual doors of the vault itself—two heavy bronze valves, meeting in the centre. Each bore a ring for a handle, pierced through a Gorgon's head embossed upon the surface. Yolande pushed them with her hand. They yielded instantly to her light touch, and opened *inward*. Yolande, still in front, passed from the glow of the moon to the gloom of the vault, which a ray of moonlight just descended obliquely. As she passed, for a second, a weird sight met Maisie's eyes. Her face and hands and dress became momentarily self-luminous; but through them, as they glowed, she could descry within every bone and joint of her living skeleton, dimly shadowed in dark through the luminous haze that marked her body.

Maisie drew back once more, terrified. Yet her terror was not quite what one could describe as fear: it was rather a vague sense of the profoundly mystical. "I can't! I can't!" she cried, with an appealing glance. "Hedda! Yolande! I cannot go with you."

Hedda held her hand tight, and almost seemed to force her. But Yolande, in front, like a mother with her child, turned round with a grave smile. "No, no," she said reprovingly. "Let her come if she will, Hedda, of her own accord, not otherwise. The tower demands a willing victim."

Her hand on Maisie's wrist was strong but persuasive. It drew her without exercising the faintest compulsion. "Will you come with us, dear?" she said, in that winning silvery tone which had captivated Maisie's fancy from the very first moment they spoke together. Maisie gazed into her eyes. They were deep and tender. A strange resolution seemed to nerve her for the effort. "Yes, yes—I—will—come—with you," she answered slowly.

Hedda on one side, Yolande on the other, now went before her, holding her wrists in their grasp, but rather enticing than drawing her. As each reached the gloom, the same luminous appearance which Maisie had noticed before spread over their bodies, and the same weird skeleton shape showed faintly through their limbs in darker shadow. Maisie crossed the threshold with a convulsive gasp. As she crossed it she looked down at her own dress and body. They were semi-transparent, like the others', though not quite so self-luminous; the framework of her limbs appeared within in less certain outline, yet quite dark and distinguishable.

The doors swung to of themselves behind her. Those three stood alone in the vault of Wolverden.

Alone, for a minute or two; and then, as her eyes grew accustomed to the grey dusk of the interior, Maisie began to perceive that the vault opened out into a large and beautiful hall or crypt, dimly lighted at first, but becoming each moment more vaguely clear and more dreamily definite. Gradually she could make out great rock-hewn pillars, Romanesque in their outline or dimly Oriental, like the sculptured columns in the caves of Ellora, supporting a roof of vague and uncertain dimensions, more or less strangely domeshaped. The effect on the whole was like that of the second impression produced by some dim cathedral, such as Chartres or Milan, after the eyes have grown accustomed to the mellow light from the stained-glass windows, and have recovered from the blinding glare of the outer sunlight. But the architecture, if one may call it so, was more mosque-like and magical. She turned to her companions. Yolande and Hedda stood still by her side; their bodies were now self-luminous to a greater

degree than even at the threshold; but the terrible
transparency had disappeared altogether; they were
once more but beautiful though strangely transfigured
and more than mortal women.

Then Maisie understood in her own soul, dimly, the
meaning of those mystic words written over the portal
—"*Mors janua vitae*"—Death is the gate of life; and
also the interpretation of that awful vision of death
dwelling within them as they crossed the threshold; for
through that gate they had passed to this underground
palace.

Her two guides still held her hands, one on either
side. But they seemed rather to lead her on now, seduc-
tively and resistlessly, than to draw or compel her. As
she moved in through the hall, with its endless vistas of
shadowy pillars, seen now behind, now in dim perspec-
tive, she was gradually aware that many other people
crowded its aisles and corridors. Slowly they took shape
as forms more or less clad, mysterious, varied, and of
many ages. Some of them wore flowing robes, half
mediaeval in shape, like the two friends who had
brought her there. They looked like the saints on a
stained-glass window. Others were girt merely with a
light and floating Coan sash; while some stood dimly
nude in the darker recesses of the temple or palace. All
leaned eagerly forward with one mind as she approached, and regarded her with deep and sympathetic
interest. A few of them murmured words—mere cab-
alistic sounds which at first she could not understand;
but as she moved further into the hall, and saw at each
step more clearly into the gloom, they began to have a
meaning for her. Before long, she was aware that she

understood the mute tumult of voices at once by some internal instinct. The Shades addressed her; she answered them. She knew by intuition what tongue they spoke; it was the Language of the Dead; and, by passing that portal with her two companions, she had herself become enabled both to speak and understand it.

A soft and flowing tongue, this speech of the Nether World—all vowels it seemed, without distinguishable consonants; yet dimly recalling every other tongue, and compounded, as it were, of what was common to all of them. It flowed from those shadowy lips as clouds issue inchoate from a mountain valley; it was formless, uncertain, vague, but yet beautiful. She hardly knew, indeed, as it fell upon her senses, if it were sound or perfume.

Through this tenuous world Maisie moved as in a dream, her two companions still cheering and guiding her. When they reached an inner shrine or chantry of the temple she was dimly conscious of more terrible forms pervading the background than any of those that had yet appeared to her. This was a more austere and antique apartment than the rest; a shadowy cloister, prehistoric in its severity; it recalled to her mind something indefinitely intermediate between the huge unwrought trilithons of Stonehenge and the massive granite pillars of Philæ and Luxor. At the further end of the sanctuary a sort of Sphinx looked down on her, smiling mysteriously. At its base, on a rude megalithic throne, in solitary state, a High Priest was seated. He bore in his hand a wand or sceptre. All round, a strange court of half-unseen acolytes and shadowy hierophants stood attentive. They were girt, as she fancied, in what looked like leopards' skins, or in the fells of some earlier prehistoric lion. These wore sabre-shaped teeth suspended by a string round their dusky necks; others had ornaments of uncut amber, or hatchets of jade threaded as collars on a cord of sinew. A few, more barbaric than savage in type, flaunted torques of gold as armlets and necklets.

The High Priest rose slowly and held out his two hands, just level with his head, the palms turned outward. "You have brought a willing victim as Guardian of the Tower?" he asked, in that mystic tongue, of Yolande and Hedda.

"We have brought a willing victim," the two girls answered.

The High Priest gazed at her. His glance was piercing. Maisie trembled less with fear than with a sense of strangeness, such as a neophyte might feel on being first presented at some courtly pageant. "You come of your own accord?" the Priest inquired of her in solemn accents.

"I come of my own accord," Maisie answered, with an inner consciousness that she was bearing her part in some immemorial ritual. Ancestral memories seemed to stir within her.

"It is well," the Priest murmured. Then he turned to her guides. "She is of royal lineage?" he inquired, taking his wand in his hand again.

"She is a Llewelyn," Yolande answered, "of royal lineage, and of the race that, after your own, earliest bore sway in this land of Britain. She has in her veins the blood of Arthur, of Ambrosius, and of Vortigern."

"It is well," the Priest said again. "I know these

princes." Then he turned to Maisie. "This is the ritual
of those who build," he said, in a very deep voice. "It
has been the ritual of those who build from the days of
the builders of Lokmariaker and Avebury. Every building man makes shall have its human soul, the soul of a
virgin to guard and protect it. Three souls it requires as
a living talisman against chance and change. One soul is
the soul of the human victim slain beneath the foundation-stone; she is the guardian spirit against earthquake
and ruin. One soul is the soul of the human victim slain
when the building is half built up; she is the guardian
spirit against battle and tempest. One soul is the soul of
the human victim who flings herself of her own free
will off tower or gable when the building is complete;
she is the guardian spirit against thunder and lightning.
Unless a building be duly fasted with these three, how
can it hope to stand against the hostile powers of fire
and flood and storm and earthquake?"

An assessor at his side, unnoticed till then, took up
the parable. He had a stern Roman face, and bore a
shadowy suit of Roman armour. "In times of old," he
said, with iron austerity, "all men knew well these rules
of building. They built in solid stone to endure for
ever: the works they erected have lasted to this day, in
this land and others. So built we the amphitheatres of
Rome and Verona; so built we the walls of Lincoln,
York, and London. In the blood of a king's son laid we
the foundation-stone: in the blood of a king's son laid
we the coping-stone: in the blood of a maiden of royal
line fasted we the bastions against fire and lightning.
But in these latter days, since faith grows dim, men
build with burnt brick and rubble of plaster; no foun-

dation spirit or guardian soul do they give to their
bridges, their walls, or their towers: so bridges break,
and walls fall in, and towers crumble, and the art and
mystery of building aright have perished from among
you."

He ceased. The High Priest held out his wand and
spoke again. "We are the Assembly of Dead Builders
and Dead Victims," he said, "for this mark of Wolverden; all of whom have built or been built upon in this
holy site of immemorial sanctity. We are the stones of a
living fabric. Before this place was a Christian church,
it was a temple of Woden. And before it was a temple
of Woden, it was a shrine of Hercules. And before it
was a shrine of Hercules, it was a grove of Nodens. And
before it was a grove of Nodens, it was a Stone Circle of
the Host of Heaven. And before it was a Stone Circle
of the Host of Heaven, it was the grave and tumulus
and underground palace of Me, who am the earliest
builder of all in this place; and my name in my ancient
tongue is Wolf, and I laid and hallowed it. And after
me, Wolf, and my namesake Wulfhere, was this barrow
called Ad Lupum and Wolverden. And all these that
are here with me have built and been built upon in this
holy site for all generations. And *you* are the last who
come to join us."

Maisie felt a cold thrill course down her spine as she
spoke these words; but courage did not fail her. She
was dimly aware that those who offer themselves as victims for service must offer themselves willingly; for the
gods demand a voluntary victim; no beast can be slain
unless it nod assent; and none can be made a guardian
spirit who takes not the post upon him of his own free

will. She turned meekly to Hedda. "Who are you?" she asked, trembling.

"I am Hedda," the girl answered, in the same soft sweet voice and winning tone as before; "Hedda, the daughter of Gorm, the chief of the Northmen who settled in East Anglia. And I was a worshipper of Thor and Odin. And when my father, Gorm, fought against Alfred, King of Wessex, was I taken prisoner. And Wulfhere, the Kenting, was then building the first church and tower of Wolverden. And they baptized me, and shrived me, and I consented of my own free will to be built under the foundation-stone. And there my body lies built up to this day; and *I* am the guardian spirit against earthquake and ruin."

"And who are you?" Maisie asked, turning again to Yolande.

"I am Yolande Fitz-Aylwin," the tall dark girl answered; "a royal maiden too, sprung from the blood of Henry Plantagenet. And when Roland Fitz-Stephen was building anew the choir and chancel of Wulfhere's minister, I chose to be immured in the fabric of the wall, for love of the Church and all holy saints; and there my body lies built up to this day; and *I* am the guardian against battle and tempest."

Maisie held her friend's hand tight. Her voice hardly trembled. "And I?" she asked once more. "What fate for me? Tell me!"

"Your task is easier far," Yolande answered gently. "For *you* shall be the guardian of the new tower against thunder and lightning. Now, those who guard against earthquake and battle are buried live under the foundation-stone or in the wall of the building;

there they die a slow death of starvation and choking. But those who guard against thunder and lightning cast themselves alive of their own free will from the battlements of the tower, and die in the air before they reach the ground; so their fate is the easiest and the lightest of all who would serve mankind; and thenceforth they live with us here in our palace."

Maisie clung to her hand still tighter. "Must I do it?" she asked, pleading.

"It is not *must,*" Yolande replied in the same caressing tone, yet with a calmness as of one in whom earthly desires and earthly passions are quenched for ever. "It is as you choose yourself. None but a willing victim may be a guardian spirit. This glorious privilege comes but to the purest and best amongst us. Yet what better end can you ask for your soul than to dwell here in our midst as our comrade for ever, where all is peace, and to preserve the tower whose guardian you are from evil assaults of lightning and thunderbolt?"

Maisie flung her arms round her friend's neck. "But —I am afraid," she murmured. Why she should even wish to consent she knew not, yet the strange serene peace in these strange girls' eyes made her mysteriously in love with them and with the fate they offered her. They seemed to move like the stars in their orbits. "How shall I leap from the top?" she cried. "How shall I have courage to mount the stairs alone, and fling myself off from the lonely battlement?"

Yolande unwound her arms with a gentle forbearance. She coaxed her as one coaxes an unwilling child. "You will *not* be alone," she said, with a tender pressure. "We will all go with you. We will help you and encourage you. We will sing our sweet songs of life-in-death to you. Why should you draw back? All we have faced it in ten thousand ages, and we tell you with one voice, you need not fear it. 'Tis life you should fear—life, with its dangers, it toils, its heartbreakings. Here we dwell for ever in unbroken peace. Come, come, and join us!"

She held out her arms with an enticing gesture. Maisie sprang into them, sobbing. "Yes, I will come," she cried in an access of hysterical fervour. "These are the arms of Death—I embrace them. These are the lips of Death—I kiss them. Yolande, Yolande, I will do as you ask me!"

The tall dark girl in the luminous white robe stooped down and kissed her twice on the forehead in return. Then she looked at the High Priest. "We are ready," she murmured in a low, grave voice. "The Victim consents. The Virgin will die. Lead on to the tower. We are ready! We are ready!"

IV

From the recesses of the temple—if temple it were—from the inmost shrines of the shrouded cavern, unearthly music began to sound of itself, with wild modulation, on strange reeds and tabors. It swept through the aisles like a rushing wind on an Æolian harp; at times it wailed with a voice like a woman's; at times it rose loud in an organ-note of triumph; at times it sank low into a pensive and melancholy flute-like symphony. It waxed and waned; it swelled and died away again; but no man saw how or whence it proceeded. Wizard echoes issued from the crannies and vents in the invisi-

ble walls; they sighed from the ghostly interspaces of
the pillars; they keened and moaned from the vast
overhanging dome of the palace. Gradually the song
shaped itself by weird stages into a processional meas-
ure. At its sound the High Priest rose slowly from his
immemorial seat on the mighty cromlech which
formed his throne. The Shades in leopards' skins
ranged themselves in bodiless rows on either hand; the
ghostly wearers of the sabre-toothed lions' fangs followed like ministrants in the footsteps of their hierarch.

Hedda and Yolande took their places in the procession. Maisie stood between the two, with hair floating
on the air; she looked like a novice who goes up to take
the veil, accompanied and cheered by two elder sisters.

The ghostly pageant began to move. Unseen music
followed it with fitful gusts of melody. They passed
down the main corridor, between shadowy Doric or
Ionic pillars which grew dimmer and ever dimmer
again in the distance as they approached, with slow
steps, the earthward portal.

At the gate, the High Priest pushed against the
valves with his hand. They opened *outward*.

He passed into the moonlight. The attendants
thronged after him. As each wild figure crossed the
threshold the same strange sight as before met Maisie's
eyes. For a second of time each ghostly body became
self-luminous, as with some curious phosphorescence;
and through each, at the moment of passing the portal,
the dim outline of a skeleton loomed briefly visible.
Next instant it had clothed itself as with earthly
members.

Maisie reached the outer air. As she did so, she

gasped. For a second, its chilliness and freshness almost choked her. She was conscious now that the atmosphere of the vault, though pleasant in its way, and warm and dry, had been loaded with fumes as of burning incense, and with somnolent vapours of poppy and mandragora. Its drowsy ether had cast her into a lethargy. But after the first minute in the outer world, the keen night air revived her. Snow lay still on the ground a little deeper than when she first came out, and the moon rode lower; otherwise, all was as before, save that only one or two lights still burned here and there in the great house on the terrace. Among them she could recognize her own room, on the ground floor in the new wing, by its open window.

The procession made its way across the churchyard towards the tower. As it wound among the graves an owl hooted. All at once Maisie remembered the lines that had so chilled her a few short hours before in the drawing-room—

> "The glow-worm o'er grave and stone
>   Shall light thee steady;
> The owl from the steeple sing,
>   'Welcome, proud lady!'"

But, marvellous to relate, they no longer alarmed her. She felt rather that a friend was welcoming her home; she clung to Yolande's hand with a gentle pressure.

As they passed in front of the porch, with its ancient yew-tree, a stealthy figure glided out like a ghost from the darkling shadow. It was a woman, bent and bowed, with quivering limbs that shook half palsied. Maisie recognized old Bessie. "I knew she would come!" the old hag muttered between her toothless jaws. "I knew Wolverden Tower would yet be duly fasted!"

She put herself, as of right, at the head of the procession. They moved on to the tower, gliding rather than walking. Old Bessie drew a rusty key from her pocket, and fitted it with a twist into the brand-new lock. "What turned the old will turn the new," she murmured, looking round and grinning. Maisie shrank from her as she shrank from not one of the Dead; but she followed on still into the ringers' room at the base of the tower.

Thence a staircase in the corner led up to the summit. The High Priest mounted the stair, chanting a mystic refrain, whose runic sounds were no longer intelligible to Maisie. As she reached the outer air, the Tongue of the Dead seemed to have become a mere blank of mingled odours and murmurs to her. It was like a summer breeze, sighing through warm and resinous pinewoods. But Yolande and Hedda spoke to her yet, to cheer her, in the language of the living. She recognized that as *revenants* they were still in touch with the upper air and the world of the embodied.

They tempted her up the stair with encouraging fingers. Maisie followed them like a child, in implicit confidence. The steps wound round and round, spirally, and the staircase was dim; but a supernatural light seemed to fill the tower, diffused from the bodies or souls of its occupants. At the head of all, the High Priest still chanted as he went his unearthly litany; magic sounds of chimes seemed to swim in unison with his tune as they mounted. Were those floating notes material or spiritual? They passed the belfry; no tongue of metal wagged; but the rims of the great bells resounded and reverberated to the ghostly symphony with sympathetic music. Still they passed on and on, upward and upward. They reached the ladder that alone gave access to the final storey. Dust and cobwebs already clung to it. Once more Maisie drew back. It was dark overhead, and the luminous haze began to fail them. Her friends held her hands with the same kindly persuasive touch as ever. "I cannot!" she cried, shrinking away from the tall, steep ladder. "Oh, Yolande, I cannot!"

"Yes, dear," Yolande whispered in a soothing voice. "You can. It is but ten steps, and I will hold your hand tight. Be brave and mount them!"

The sweet voice encouraged her. It was like heavenly music. She knew not why she should submit, or, rather, consent; but none the less she consented. Some spell seemed cast over her. With tremulous feet, scarcely realizing what she did, she mounted the ladder and went up four steps of it.

Then she turned and looked down again. Old Bessie's wrinkled face met her frightened eyes. It was smiling horribly. She shrank back once more, terrified. "I can't do it," she cried, "if that woman comes up! I'm not afraid of *you,* dear"—she pressed Yolande's hand —"but she, she is too terrible!"

Hedda looked back and raised a warning finger. "Let the woman stop below," she said; "she savours too much of the evil world. We must do nothing to frighten the willing victim."

The High Priest by this time, with his ghostly fingers, had opened the trap-door that gave access to the sum-

mit. A ray of moonlight slanted through the aperture.
The breeze blew down with it. Once more Maisie felt
the stimulating and reviving effect of the open air.
Vivified by its freshness, she struggled up to the top,
passed out through the trap, and found herself standing
on the open platform at the summit of the tower.

The moon had not yet quite set. The light on the
snow shone pale green and mysterious. For miles and
miles around she could just make out, by its aid, the
dim contour of the downs, with their thin white man-
tle, in the solemn silence. Range behind range rose
faintly shimmering. The chant had now ceased; the
High Priest and his acolytes were mingling strange
herbs in a mazar-bowl or chalice. Stray perfumes of
myrrh and of cardamoms were wafted towards her.
The men in leopards' skins burnt smouldering sticks of
spikenard. Then Yolande led the postulant forward
again, and placed her close up to the new white parapet. Stone heads of virgins smiled on her from the angles. "She must front the east," Hedda said in a tone of
authority: and Yolande turned her face towards the
rising sun accordingly. Then she opened her lips and
spoke in a very solemn voice. "From this new-built
tower you fling yourself," she said, or rather intoned,
"that you may serve mankind, and all the powers that
be, as its guardian spirit against thunder and lightning.
Judged a virgin, pure and unsullied in deed and word
and thought, of royal race and ancient lineage—a
Cymry of the Cymry—you are found worthy to be in-
trusted with this charge and this honour. Take care
that never shall dart or thunderbolt assault this tower,
as She that is below you takes care to preserve it from

earthquake and ruin, and She that is midway takes care to preserve it from battle and tempest. This is your charge. See well that you keep it."

She took her by both hands. "Mary Llewelyn," she said, "you willing victim, step on to the battlement."

Maisie knew not why, but with very little shrinking she stepped as she was told, by the aid of a wooden footstool, on to the eastward-looking parapet. There, in her loose white robe, with her arms spread abroad, and her hair flying free, she poised herself for a second, as if about to shake out some unseen wings and throw herself on the air like a swift or a swallow.

"Mary Llewelyn," Yolande said once more, in a still deeper tone, with ineffable earnestness, "cast yourself down, a willing sacrifice, for the service of man, and the security of this tower against thunderbolt and lightning."

Maisie stretched her arms wider, and leaned forward in act to leap, from the edge of the parapet, on to the snow-clad churchyard.

V

One second more and the sacrifice would have been complete. But before she could launch herself from the tower, she felt suddenly a hand laid upon her shoulder from behind to restrain her. Even in her existing state of nervous exaltation she was aware at once that it was the hand of a living and solid mortal, not that of a soul or guardian spirit. It lay heavier upon her than Hedda's or Yolande's. It seemed to clog and burden her. With a violent effort she strove to shake herself free, and carry out her now fixed intention of self-immolation, for the safety of the tower. But the hand was too strong for her. She could not shake it off. It gripped and held her.

She yielded, and, reeling, fell back with a gasp on to the platform of the tower. At the selfsame moment a strange terror and commotion seemed to seize all at once on the assembled spirits. A weird cry rang voiceless through the shadowy company. Maisie heard it as in a dream, very dim and distant. It was thin as a bat's note; almost inaudible to the ear, yet perceived by the brain or at least by the spirit. It was a cry of alarm, of fright, of warning. With one accord, all the host of phantoms rushed hurriedly forward to the battlements and pinnacles. The ghostly High Priest went first, with his wand held downward; the men in leopards' skins and other assistants followed in confusion. Theirs was a reckless rout. They flung themselves from the top, like fugitives from a cliff, and floated fast through the air on invisible pinions. Hedda and Yolande, ambassadresses and intermediaries with the upper air, were the last to fly from the living presence. They clasped her hand silently, and looked deep into her eyes. There was something in that calm yet regretful look that seemed to say, "Farewell! We have tried in vain to save you, sister, from the terrors of living."

The horde of spirits floated away on the air, as in a witches' Sabbath, to the vault whence it issued. The doors swung on their rusty hinges, and closed behind them. Maisie stood alone with the hand that grasped her on the tower.

The shock of the grasp, and the sudden departure of the ghostly band in such wild dismay, threw Maisie for a while into a state of semi-unconsciousness. Her head reeled round; her brain swam faintly. She clutched for support at the parapet of the tower. But the hand that held her sustained her still. She felt herself gently drawn down with quiet mastery, and laid on the stone floor close by the trap-door that led to the ladder.

The next thing of which she could feel sure was the voice of the Oxford undergraduate. He was distinctly frightened and not a little tremulous. "I think," he said very softly, laying her head on his lap, "you had better rest a while, Miss Llewelyn, before you try to get down again. I hope I didn't catch you and disturb you too hastily. But one step more, and you would have been over the edge. I really couldn't help it."

"Let me go," Maisie moaned, trying to raise herself again, but feeling too faint and ill to make the necessary effort to recover the power of motion. "I *want* to go with them! I *want* to join them!"

"Some of the others will be up before long," the undergraduate said, supporting her head in his hands; "and they'll help me to get you down again. Mr. Yates is in the belfry. Meanwhile, if I were you, I'd lie quite still, and take a drop or two of this brandy."

He held it to her lips. Maisie drank a mouthful, hardly knowing what she did. Then she lay quiet where he placed her for some minutes. How they lifted her down and conveyed her to her bed she scarcely knew. She was dazed and terrified. She could only remember afterward that three or four gentlemen in roughly huddled clothes had carried or handed her down the ladder between them. The spiral stair and all the rest were a blank to her.

VI

When she next awoke she was lying in her bed in the same room at the Hall, with Mrs. West by her side, leaning over her tenderly.

Maisie looked up through her closed eyes and just saw the motherly face and grey hair bending above her. Then voices came to her from the mist, vaguely: "Yesterday was so hot for the time of year, you see!" "Very unusual weather, of course, for Christmas." "But a thunderstorm! So strange! I put it down to that. The electrical disturbance must have affected the poor child's head." Then it dawned upon her that the conversation she heard was passing between Mrs. West and a doctor.

She raised herself suddenly and wildly on her arms. The bed faced the windows. She looked out and beheld —the tower of Wolverden church, split from top to bottom with a mighty rent, while half its height lay tossed in fragments on the ground in the churchyard.

"What is it?" she cried wildly, with a flush as of shame.

"Hush, hush!" the doctor said. "Don't trouble! Don't look at it!"

"Was it—after I came down?" Maisie moaned in vague terror.

The doctor nodded. "An hour after you were brought down," he said, "a thunderstorm broke over it.

The lightning struck and shattered the tower. They had not yet put up the lightning-conductor. It was to have been done on Boxing Day."

A weird remorse possessed Maisie's soul. "My fault!" she cried, starting up. "My fault, my fault! I have neglected my duty!"

"Don't talk," the doctor answered, looking hard at her. "It is always dangerous to be too suddenly aroused from these curious overwrought sleeps and trances."

"And old Bessie?" Maisie exclaimed, trembling with an eerie presentiment.

The doctor glanced at Mrs. West. "How did she know?" he whispered. Then he turned to Maisie. "You may as well be told the truth as suspect it," he said slowly. "Old Bessie must have been watching there. She was crushed and half buried beneath the falling tower."

"One more question, Mrs. West," Maisie murmured, growing faint with an access of supernatural fear. "Those two nice girls who sat on the chairs at each side of me through the tableaux—are they hurt? Were they in it?"

Mrs. West soothed her hand. "My dear child," she said gravely, with quiet emphasis, "there were *no* other girls. This is mere hallucination. You sat alone by yourself through the whole of the evening."

Tarnhelm

HUGH WALPOLE

Home for the holidays? We all do go home or we all should, said Dickens.

It is the time to get away from our everyday selves and take a holiday of the imagination.

So let's spend a Christmas holiday with a young boy almost homeless until he is taken in that Christmas by those uncles. Hugh Walpole was a master at wielding a weird pen. Over this story hang all sorts of primitive feelings about the winter solstice and the early Christmas folklore and legends of Walpole's countryside.

The Christmas period was not just a time of ghosts; it was a time of other strange apparitions—monsters. In rural areas childhood could be frightened by seeing creatures whose tracks were barely distinguishable in the snow, strange creatures that were bred from strange, almost pagan, beliefs. A holiday of horror indeed.

I WAS, I SUPPOSE, at that time a peculiar child, peculiar a little by nature, but also because I had spent so much of my young life in the company of people very much older than myself.

After the events that I am now going to relate, some quite indelible mark was set on me. I became then, and have always been since, one of those persons, otherwise insignificant, who have decided, without possibility of change, about certain questions.

Some things, doubted by most of the world, are for these people true and beyond argument; this certainty of theirs gives them a kind of stamp, as though they lived so much in their imagination as to have very little assurance as to what is fact and what fiction. This "oddness" of theirs puts them apart. If now, at the age of fifty, I am a man with very few friends, very much alone, it is because, if you like, my Uncle Robert died in a strange manner forty years ago and I was a witness of his death.

I have never until now given any account of the strange proceedings that occurred at Faildyke Hall on the evening of Christmas Eve in the year 1890. The incidents of that evening are still remembered very clearly by one or two people, and a kind of legend of my Uncle Robert's death has been carried on into the younger generation. But no one still alive was a witness of them as I was, and I feel it is time that I set them down upon paper.

I write them down without comment. I extenuate nothing; I disguise nothing. I am not, I hope, in any way a vindictive man, but my brief meeting with my Uncle Robert and the circumstances of his death gave

my life, even at that early age, a twist difficult for me
very readily to forgive.

As to the so-called supernatural element in my story,
everyone must judge for himself about that. We deride
or we accept according to our natures. If we are built
of a certain solid practical material the probability is
that no evidence, however definite, however first-hand,
will convince us. If dreams are our daily portion, one
dream more or less will scarcely shake our sense of reality.

However, to my story.

My father and mother were in India from my eighth
to my thirteenth years. I did not see them, except on
two occasions when they visited England. I was an only
child, loved dearly by both my parents, who, however,
loved one another yet more. They were an exceedingly
sentimental couple of the old-fashioned kind. My father was in the Indian Civil Service, and wrote poetry.
He even had his epic, *Tantalus: A Poem in Four
Cantos,* published at his own expense.

This, added to the fact that my mother had been
considered an invalid before he married her, made my
parents feel that they bore a very close resemblance to
the Brownings, and my father even had a pet name for
my mother that sounded curiously like the famous and
hideous "Ba."

I was a delicate child, was sent to Mr. Ferguson's
Private Academy at the tender age of eight, and spent
my holidays as the rather unwanted guest of various
relations.

"Unwanted" because I was, I imagine, a difficult
child to understand. I had an old grandmother who

lived at Folkestone, two aunts who shared a little house in Kensington, an aunt, uncle and a brood of cousins inhabiting Cheltenham, and two uncles who lived in Cumberland. All these relations, except the two uncles, had their proper share of me and for none of them had I any great affection.

Children were not studied in those days as they are now. I was thin, pale and bespectacled, aching for affection but not knowing at all how to obtain it; outwardly undemonstrative but inwardly emotional and sensitive, playing games, because of my poor sight, very badly, reading a great deal more than was good for me, and telling myself stories all day and part of every night.

All of my relations tired of me, I fancy, in turn, and at last it was decided that my uncles in Cumberland must do their share. These two were my father's brothers, the eldest of a long family of which he was the youngest. My Uncle Robert, I understood, was nearly seventy, my Uncle Constance some five years younger. I remember always thinking that Constance was a funny name for a man.

My Uncle Robert was the owner of Faildyke Hall, a country house between the lake of Wastwater and the little town of Seascale on the sea coast. Uncle Constance had lived with Uncle Robert for many years. It was decided, after some family correspondence, that the Christmas of this year, 1890, should be spent by me at Faildyke Hall.

I was at this time just eleven years old, thin and skinny, with a bulging forehead, large spectacles and a nervous, shy manner. I always set out, I remember, on

any new adventures with mingled emotions of terror
and anticipation. Maybe *this* time the miracle would
occur: I should discover a friend or a fortune, should
cover myself with glory in some unexpected way; be at
last what I always longed to be, a hero.

I was glad that I was not going to any of my other
relations for Christmas, and especially not to my
cousins at Cheltenham, who teased and persecuted me
and were never free of earsplitting noises. What I
wanted most in life was to be allowed to read in peace.
I understood that at Faildyke there was a glorious library.

My aunt saw me into the train. I had been presented
by my uncle with one of the most gory of Harrison
Ainsworth's romances, "The Lancashire Witches," and
I had five bars of chocolate cream, so that that journey
was as blissfully happy as any experience could be to
me at that time. I was permitted to read in peace, and
I had just then little more to ask of life.

Nevertheless, as the train puffed its way north, this
new country began to force itself on my attention. I had
never before been in the North of England, and I was
not prepared for the sudden sense of space and
freshness that I received.

The naked, unsystematic hills, the freshness of the
wind on which the birds seemed to be carried with es-
pecial glee, the stone walls that ran like grey ribbons
about the moors, and, above all, the vast expanse of sky
upon whose surface clouds swam, raced, eddied and extended as I had never anywhere witnessed. . . .

I sat, lost and absorbed, at my carriage window, and
when at last, long after dark had fallen, I heard "Sea-

scale" called by the porter, I was still staring in a sort of romantic dream. When I stepped out on to the little narrow platform and was greeted by the salt tang of the sea wind my first real introduction to the North Country may be said to have been completed. I am writing now in another part of that same Cumberland country, and beyond my window the line of the fell runs strong and bare against the sky, while below it the Lake lies, a fragment of silver glass at the feet of Skiddaw.

It may be that my sense of the deep mystery of this country had its origin in this same strange story that I am now relating. But again perhaps not, for I believe that that first evening arrival at Seascale worked some change in me, so that since then none of the world's beauties—from the crimson waters of Kashmir to the rough glories of our own Cornish coast—can rival for me the sharp, peaty winds and strong, resilient turf of the Cumberland hills.

That was a magical drive in the pony-trip to Faildyke that evening. It was bitterly cold, but I did not seem to mind it. Everything was magical to me.

From the first I could see the great slow hump of Black Combe jet against the frothy clouds of the winter night, and I could hear the sea breaking and the soft rustle of the bare twigs in the hedgerows.

I made, too, the friend of my life that night, for it was Bob Armstrong who was driving the trap. He has often told me since (for although he is a slow man of few words he likes to repeat the things that seem to him worth while) that I struck him as "pitifully lost" that evening on the Seascale platform. I looked, I don't doubt, pinched and cold enough. In any case it was a lucky appearance for me, for I won Armstrong's heart there and then, and he, once he gave it, could never bear to take it back again.

He, on his side, seemed to me gigantic that night. He had, I believe, one of the broadest chests in the world: it was a curse to him, he said, because no ready-made shirts would ever suit him.

I sat in close to him because of the cold; he was very warm, and I could feel his heart beating like a steady clock inside his rough coat. It beat for me that night, and it has beaten for me, I'm glad to say, ever since.

In truth, as things turned out, I needed a friend. I was nearly asleep and stiff all over my little body when I was handed down from the trap and at once led into what seemed to me an immense hall crowded with the staring heads of slaughtered animals and smelling of straw.

I was so sadly weary that my uncles, when I met them in a vast billiard-room in which a great fire roared in a stone fireplace like a demon, seemed to me to be double.

In any case, what an odd pair they were! My Uncle Robert was a little man with grey untidy hair and little sharp eyes hooded by two of the bushiest eyebrows known to humanity. He wore (I remember as though it were yesterday) shabby country clothes of a faded green colour, and he had on one finger a ring with a thick red stone.

Another thing that I noticed at once when he kissed me (I detested to be kissed by anybody) was a faint scent that he had, connected at once in my mind with the caraway-seeds that there are in seed-cake. I noticed, too, that his teeth were discoloured with yellow.

My Uncle Constance I liked at once. He was fat, round, friendly and clean. Rather a dandy was Uncle Constance. He wore a flower in his buttonhole and his linen was snowy white in contrast with his brother's.

I noticed one thing, though, at that very first meeting, and that was that before he spoke to me and put his fat arm around my shoulder he seemed to look towards his brother as though for permission. You may say that it was unusual for a boy of my age to notice so much, but in fact I noticed everything at that time. Years and laziness, alas! have slackened my observation.

II

I had a horrible dream that night; it woke me screaming, and brought Bob Armstrong in to quiet me.

My room was large, like all the other rooms that I had seen, and empty, with a great expanse of floor and a stone fireplace like the one in the billiard-room. It was, I afterwards found, next to the servants' quarters. Armstrong's room was next to mine, and Mrs. Spender's, the housekeeper's, beyond his.

Armstrong was then, and is yet, a bachelor. He used to tell me that he loved so many women that he never could bring his mind to choose any one of them. And now he has been too long my personal bodyguard and is too lazily used to my ways to change his condition. He is, moreover, seventy years of age.

Well, what I saw in my dream was this. They had lit a fire for me (and it was necessary; the room was of an icy coldness) and I dreamt that I awoke to see the flames rise to a last vigour before they died away. In the brilliance of that illumination I was conscious that something was moving in the room. I heard the movement for some little while before I saw anything.

I sat up, my heart hammering, and then to my horror discerned, slinking against the farther wall, the evillest-looking yellow mongrel of a dog that you can fancy.

I find it difficult, I have always found it difficult, to describe exactly the horror of that yellow dog. It lay partly in its colour, which was vile, partly in its mean and bony body, but for the most part in its evil head—flat, with sharp little eyes and jagged yellow teeth.

As I looked at it, it bared those teeth at me and then began to creep, with an indescribably loathsome action, in the direction of my bed. I was at first stiffened with terror. Then, as it neared the bed, its little eyes fixed upon me and its teeth bared, I screamed again and again.

The next I knew was that Armstrong was sitting on my bed, his strong arm about my trembling little body. All I could say over and over was, "The Dog! the Dog! the Dog!"

He soothed me as though he had been my mother.

"See, there's no dog there! There's no one but me! There's no one but me!"

I continued to tremble, so he got into bed with me, held me close to him, and it was in his comforting arms that I fell asleep.

III

In the morning I woke to a fresh breeze and a shining sun and the chrysanthemums, orange, crimson and

dun, blowing against the grey stone wall beyond the
sloping lawns. So I forgot about my dream. I only knew
that I loved Bob Armstrong better than anyone else on
earth.

Everyone during the next days was very kind to me. I
was so deeply excited by this country, so new to me,
that at first I could think of nothing else. Bob
Armstrong was Cumbrian from the top of his flaxen
head to the thick nails under his boots, and, in grunts
and monosyllables, as was his way, he gave me the
colour of the ground.

There was romance everywhere: smugglers stealing
in and out of Drigg and Seascale, the ancient Cross in
Gosforth churchyard, Ravenglass, with all its seabirds,
once a port of splendour.

Muncaster Castle and Broughton and black Wastwater with the grim Screes, Black Combe, upon whose
broad back the shadows were always dancing—even
the little station at Seascale, naked to the sea-winds, at
whose bookstalls I bought a publication entitled the
Weekly Telegraph that contained, week by week, in-
stalments of the most thrilling story in the world.

Everywhere romance—the cows moving along the
sandy lanes, the sea thundering along the Drigg beach,
Gable and Scafell pulling their cloud-caps about their
heads, the slow voices of the Cumbrian farmers calling
their animals, the little tinkling bell of the Gosforth
church—everywhere romance and beauty.

Soon, though, as I became better accustomed to the
country, the people immediately around me began to
occupy my attention, stimulate my restless curiosity,

and especially my two uncles. They were, in fact, queer enough.

Faildyke Hall itself was not queer, only very ugly. It had been built about 1830, I should imagine, a square white building, like a thick-set, rather conceited woman with a very plain face. The rooms were large, the passages innumerable, and everything covered with a very hideous whitewash. Against this whitewash hung old photographs yellowed with age, and faded, bad water-colours. The furniture was strong and ugly.

One romantic feature, though, there was—and that was the little Grey Tower where my Uncle Robert lived. This Tower was at the end of the garden and looked out over a sloping field to the Scafell group beyond Wastwater. It had been built hundreds of years ago as a defence against the Scots. Robert had had his study and bedroom there for many years and it was his domain; no one was allowed to enter it save his old servant Hucking, a bent, wizened, grubby little man who spoke to no one and, so they said in the kitchen, managed to go through life without sleeping. He looked after my Uncle Robert, cleaned his rooms, and was supposed to clean his clothes.

I, being both an inquisitive and romantic-minded boy, was soon as eagerly excited about this Tower as was Bluebeard's wife about the forbidden room. Bob told me that whatever I did I was never to set foot inside.

And then I discovered another thing—that Bob Armstrong hated, feared and was proud of my Uncle Robert. He was proud of him because he was head of the family, and because, so he said, he was the cleverest old man in the world.

"Nothing he can't seemingly do," said Bob, "but he don't like you to watch him at it."

All this only increased my longing to see the inside of the Tower, although I couldn't be said to be fond of my Uncle Robert either.

It would be hard to say that I disliked him during those first days. He was quite kindly to me when he met me, and at meal-times, when I sat with my two uncles at the long table in the big, bare, whitewashed dining-room, he was always anxious to see that I had plenty to eat. But I never liked him; it was perhaps because he wasn't clean. Children are sensitive to those things. Perhaps I didn't like the fusty, seed-caky smell that he carried about with him.

Then there came the day when he invited me into the Grey Tower and told me about Tarnhelm.

Pale slanting shadows of sunlight fell across the chrysanthemums and the grey stone walls, the long fields and the dusky hills. I was playing by myself by the little stream that ran beyond the rose garden, when Uncle Robert came up behind me in the soundless way he had, and, tweaking me by the ear, asked me whether I would like to come with him inside his Tower. I was, of course, eager enough; but I was frightened too, especially when I saw Hucking's moth-eaten old countenance peering at us from one of the narrow slits that pretended to be windows.

However, in we went, my hand in Uncle Robert's hot dry one. There wasn't, in reality, so very much to see when you were inside—all untidy and musty, with

cobwebs over the doorways and old pieces of rusty iron
and empty boxes in the corners, and the long table in
Uncle Robert's study covered with a thousand things—
books with the covers hanging on them, sticky green
bottles, a looking-glass, a pair of scales, a globe, a cage
with mice in it, a statue of a naked woman, an hour-
glass—everything old and stained and dusty.

However, Uncle Robert made me sit down close to
him, and told me many interesting stories. Among
others the story about Tarnhelm.

Tarnhelm was something that you put over your
head, and its magic turned you into any animal that
you wished to be. Uncle Robert told me the story of a
god called Wotan, and how he teased the dwarf who
possessed Tarnhelm by saying that he couldn't turn
himself into a mouse or some such animal; and the
dwarf, his pride wounded, turned himself into a mouse,
which the god easily captured and so stole Tarnhelm.

On the table, among all the litter, was a grey skull-
cap.

"That's my Tarnhelm," said Uncle Robert, laughing. "Like to see me put it on?"

But I was suddenly frightened, terribly frightened.
The sight of Uncle Robert made me feel quite ill. The
room began to run round and round. The white mice in
the cage twittered. It was stuffy in that room, enough
to turn any boy sick.

IV

That was the moment, I think, when Uncle Robert
stretched out his hand towards his grey skull-cap—
after that I was never happy again in Faildyke Hall.

That action of his, simple and apparently friendly though it was, seemed to open my eyes to a number of things.

We were now within ten days of Christmas. The thought of Christmas had then—and, to tell the truth, still has—a most happy effect on me. There is the beautiful story, the geniality and kindliness, still, in spite of modern pessimists much happiness and goodwill. Even now I yet enjoy giving presents and receiving them— then it was an ecstasy to me, the look of the parcel, the paper, the string, the exquisite surprise.

Therefore I had been anticipating Christmas eagerly. I had been promised a trip into Whitehaven for present-buying, and there was to be a tree and a dance for the Gosforth villagers. Then after my visit to Uncle Robert's Tower, all my happiness of anticipation vanished. As the days went on and my observation of one thing and another developed, I would, I think, have run away back to my aunts in Kensington, had it not been for Bob Armstrong.

It was, in fact, Armstrong who started me on that voyage of observation that ended so horribly, for when he had heard that Uncle Robert had taken me inside his Tower his anger was fearful. I had never before seen him angry; now his great body shook, and he caught me and held me until I cried out.

He wanted me to promise that I would never go inside there again. What? Not even with Uncle Robert? No, most especially not with Uncle Robert; and then, dropping his voice and looking around him to be sure that there was no one listening, he began to curse Uncle Robert. This amazed me, because loyalty to his masters was one of Bob's great laws. I can see us now, standing on the stable cobbles in the falling white dusk while the horses stamped in their stalls, and the little sharp stars appeared one after another glittering between the driving clouds.

"I'll not stay," I heard him say to himself. "I'll be like the rest. I'll not be staying. To bring a child into it. . . ."

From that moment he seemed to have me very specially in his charge. Even when I could not see him I felt that his kindly eye was upon me, and this sense of the necessity that I should be guarded made me yet more uneasy and distressed.

The next thing that I observed was that the servants were all fresh, had been there not more than a month or two. Then, only a week before Christmas, the housekeeper departed. Uncle Constance seemed greatly upset at these occurrences; Uncle Robert did not seem in the least affected by them.

I come now to my Uncle Constance. At this distance of time it is strange with what clarity I still can see him—his stoutness, his shining cleanliness, his dandyism, the flower in his buttonhole, his little brilliantly shod feet, his thin, rather feminine voice. He would have been kind to me, I think, had he dared, but something kept him back. And what that something was I soon discovered; it was fear of my Uncle Robert.

It did not take me a day to discover that he was utterly subject to his brother. He said nothing without looking to see how Uncle Robert took it; suggested no plan until he first had assurance from his brother; was terrified beyond anything that I had before witnessed in a human being at any sign of irritation in my uncle.

I discovered after this that Uncle Robert enjoyed

greatly to play on his brother's fears. I did not understand enough of their life to realize what were the
weapons that Robert used, but that they were sharp
and piercing I was neither too young nor too ignorant
to perceive.

Such was our situation, then, a week before Christmas. The weather had become very wild, with a great
wind. All nature seemed in an uproar. I could fancy
when I lay in my bed at night and heard the shouting
in my chimney that I could catch the crash of the
waves upon the beach, see the black waters of Wastwater cream and curdle under the Screes. I would lie
awake and long for Bob Armstrong—the strength of his
arm and the warmth of his breast—but I considered
myself too grown a boy to make any appeal.

I remember that now almost minute by minute my
fears increased. What gave them force and power who
can say? I was much alone, I had now a great terror of
my uncle, the weather was wild, the rooms of the house
large and desolate, the servants mysterious, the walls of
the passages lit always with an unnatural glimmer because of their white colour, and although Armstrong
had watch over me he was busy in his affairs and could
not always be with me.

I grew to fear and dislike my Uncle Robert more and
more. Hatred and fear of him seemed to be everywhere, and yet he was always soft-voiced and kindly.
Then, a few days before Christmas, occurred the event
that was to turn my terror into panic.

I had been reading in the library Mrs. Radcliffe's
"Romance of the Forest," an old book long forgotten,
worthy of revival. The library was a fine room run to

seed, bookcases from floor to ceiling, the windows small and dark, holes in the old faded carpet. A lamp burnt at a distant table. One stood on a little shelf at my side.

Something, I know not what, made me look up. What I saw then can even now stamp my heart in its recollection. By the library door, not moving, staring across the room's length at me, was a yellow dog.

I will not attempt to describe all the pitiful fear and mad freezing terror that caught and held me. My main thought, I fancy, was that that other vision on my first night in the place had not been a dream. I was not asleep now; the book which I had been reading had fallen to the floor; the lamps shed their glow, I could hear the ivy tapping on the pane. No, this was reality.

The dog lifted a long, horrible leg and scratched itself. Then very slowly and silently across the carpet it came towards me.

I could not scream; I could not move; I waited. The animal was even more evil than it had seemed before, with its flat head, its narrow eyes, its yellow fangs. It came steadily in my direction, stopped once to scratch itself again, then was almost at my chair.

It looked at me, bared its fangs, but now as though it grinned at me, then passed on. After it was gone there was a thick foetid scent in the air—the scent of caraway-seed.

V

I think now on looking back that it was remarkable enough that I, a pale, nervous child who trembled at every sound, should have met the situation as I did. I said nothing about the dog to any living soul, not even to Bob Armstrong. I had my fears—and fears of a beastly and sickening kind they were, too—within my breast. I had the intelligence to perceive—and *how* I caught in the air the awareness of this I can't, at this distance, understand—that I was playing my little part in the climax to something that had been piling up, for many a month, like the clouds over Gable.

Understand that I offer from first to last in this no kind of explanation. There is possibly—and to this day I cannot quite be sure—nothing to explain. My Uncle Robert died simply—but you shall hear.

What was beyond any doubt or question was that it was after my seeing the dog in the library that Uncle Robert changed so strangely in his behaviour to me. That may have been the merest coincidence. I only know that as one grows older one calls things coincidence more and more seldom.

In any case, that same night at dinner Uncle Robert seemed twenty years older. He was bent, shrivelled, would not eat, snarled at anyone who spoke to him and especially avoided even looking at me. It was a painful meal, and it was after it, when Uncle Constance and I were sitting alone in the old yellow-papered drawing-room—a room with two ticking clocks for ever racing one another—that the most extraordinary thing occurred. Uncle Constance and I were playing draughts. The only sounds were the roaring of the wind down the chimney, the hiss and splutter of the fire, the silly ticking of the clocks. Suddenly Uncle Constance put down the piece that he was about to move and began to cry.

To a child it is always a terrible thing to see a grown-up person cry, and even to this day to hear a man cry is very distressing to me. I was moved desperately by poor Uncle Constance, who sat there, his head in his white plump hand, all his stout body shaking. I ran over to him and he clutched me as though he would never let me go. He sobbed incoherent words about protecting me, caring for me . . . seeing that that monster. . . .

At the word I remember that I too began to tremble. I asked my uncle what monster, but he could only continue to murmur incoherently about hate and not having the pluck, and if only he had the courage. . . .

Then, recovering a little, he began to ask me questions. Where had I been? Had I been into his brother's Tower? Had I seen anything that frightened me? If I did would I at once tell him? And then he muttered that he would never have allowed me to come had he known that it would go as far as this, that it would be better if I went away that night, and that if he were not afraid. . . . Then he began to tremble again and to look at the door, and I trembled too. He held me in his arms; then we thought that there was a sound and we listened, our heads up, our hearts hammering. But it was only the clocks ticking and the wind shrieking as though it would tear the house to pieces.

That night, however, when Bob Armstrong came up to bed he found me sheltering there. I whispered to him that I was frightened; I put my arms around his neck and begged him not to send me away; he promised me that I should not leave him and I slept all night in the protection of his strength.

How, though, can I give any true picture of the fear that pursued me now? For I knew from what both Armstrong and Uncle Constance had said that there

was real danger, that it was no hysterical fancy of mine
or ill-digested dream. It made it worse that Uncle Robert was now no more seen. He was sick; he kept within
his Tower, cared for by his old wizened manservant.
And so, being nowhere, he was everywhere. I stayed
with Armstrong when I could, but a kind of pride
prevented me from clinging like a girl to his coat.

A deathly silence seemed to fall about the place. No
one laughed or sang, no dog barked, no bird sang. Two
days before Christmas an iron frost came to grip the
land. The fields were rigid, the sky itself seemed to be
frozen grey, and under the olive cloud Scafell and
Gable were black.

Christmas Eve came.

On that morning, I remember, I was trying to draw
—some childish picture of one of Mrs. Radcliffe's
scenes—when the double doors unfolded and Uncle
Robert stood there. He stood there, bent, shrivelled, his
long, grey locks falling over his collar, his bushy eyebrows thrust forward. He wore his old green suit and
on his finger gleamed his heavy red ring. I was frightened, of course, but also I was touched with pity. He
looked so old, so frail, so small in this large empty
house.

I sprang up. "Uncle Robert," I asked timidly, "are
you better?"

He bent still lower until he was almost on his hands
and feet; then he looked up at me, and his yellow teeth
were bared, almost as an animal snarls. Then the doors
closed again.

The slow, stealthy, grey afternoon came at last. I
walked with Armstrong to Gosforth village on some

business that he had. We said no word of any matter at
the Hall. I told him, he has reminded me, of how fond
I was of him and that I wanted to be with him always,
and he answered that perhaps it might be so, little
knowing how true that prophecy was to stand. Like all
children I had a great capacity for forgetting the atmosphere that I was not at that moment in, and I
walked beside Bob along the frozen roads, with some of
my fears surrendered.

But not for long. It was dark when I came into the
long, yellow drawing-room. I could hear the bells of
Gosforth church pealing as I passed from the ante-
room.

A moment later there came a shrill, terrified cry:
"Who's that? Who is it?"

It was Uncle Constance, who was standing in front
of the yellow silk window curtains, staring at the dusk.
I went over to him and he held me close to him.

"Listen!" he whispered. "What can you hear?"

The double doors through which I had come were
half open. At first I could hear nothing but the clocks,
the very faint rumble of a cart on the frozen road.
There was no wind.

My uncle's fingers gripped my shoulder. "Listen!" he
said again. And now I heard. On the stone passage beyond the drawing-room was the patter of an animal's
feet. Uncle Constance and I looked at one another. In
that exchanged glance we confessed that our secret was
the same. We knew what we should see.

A moment later it was there, standing in the double
doorway, crouching a little and staring at us with a
hatred that was mad and sick—the hatred of a sick ani-

mal crazy with unhappiness, but loathing us more than
its own misery.

Slowly it came towards us, and to my reeling fancy
all the room seemed to stink of caraway-seed.

"Keep back! Keep away!" my uncle screamed.

I became oddly in my turn the protector.

"It shan't touch you! It shan't touch you, uncle!" I
called.

But the animal came on.

It stayed for a moment near a little round table that
contained a composition of dead waxen fruit under a
glass dome. It stayed here, its nose down, smelling the
ground. Then, looking up at us, it came on again.

Oh, God!—even now as I write after all these years
it is with me again, the flat skull, the cringing body in
its evil colour and that loathsome smell. It slobbered a
little at its jaw. It bared its fangs.

Then I screamed, hid my face in my uncle's breast
and saw that he held, in his trembling hand, a thick,
heavy, old-fashioned revolver.

Then he cried out:

"Go back, Robert. . . . Go back!"

The animal came on. He fired. The detonation shook
the room. The dog turned and, blood dripping from its
throat, crawled across the floor.

By the door it halted, turned and looked at us. Then
it disappeared into the other room.

My uncle had flung down the revolver; he was cry-
ing, sniffling; he kept stroking my forehead, murmuring
words.

At last, clinging to one another, we followed the

splotches of blood, across the carpet, beside the door, through the doorway.

Huddled against a chair in the outer sitting-room, one leg twisted under him, was my Uncle Robert, shot through the throat.

On the floor, by his side, was a grey skull-cap.

A Christmas Carol

CHARLES DICKENS.

*Charles Dickens and Christmas—the two are insepa-
rable. "Have you ever read those Christmas tales of
Dickens'?" Robert Louis Stevenson asked a friend? "I
have cried my eyes out. Had a terrible fight not to sob.
Oh, dear God, they are* good*—and I feel so good after
them—I shall do good and lose no time—I want to go
out and comfort someone—I* shall *give money. Oh,
what a jolly thing it is for a man to have written books
like these and just fill people's hearts with pity."*

*Dickens succeeded in filling hearts not only with pity
but with a renewal of Christmas itself. Of course, he
was obsessed by Christmas. Christmas dinners, Christmas trees, the look on the faces of the children, the fire,
the empty seats of other years, the snow, the running
home, the crisp and frosty grass, the gray slate-colored
twilight, and the stories! So he wrote the greatest of all
Christmas stories.*

Here is the best of Christmas, A Christmas Carol, *in*

the very cleverly abbreviated version that Dickens himself used in his ever-popular dramatic readings.

Stave One: MARLEY'S GHOST

MARLEY WAS DEAD, to begin with. There is no doubt whatever about that. The register of his burial was signed by the clergyman, the clerk, the undertaker, and the chief mourner. Scrooge signed it. And Scrooge's name was good upon 'Change for anything he chose to put his hand to.

Old Marley was as dead as a door-nail.

Scrooge knew he was dead? Of course he did. How could it be otherwise? Scrooge and he were partners for I don't know how many years. Scrooge was his sole executor, his sole administrator, his sole assign, his sole residuary legatee, his sole friend, his sole mourner.

Scrooge never painted out old Marley's name, however. There it yet stood, years afterwards, above the warehouse door—Scrooge and Marley. The firm was known as Scrooge and Marley. Sometimes people new to the business called Scrooge Scrooge, and sometimes Marley. He answered to both names. It was all the same to him.

Oh! But he was a tight-fisted hand at the grindstone, was Scrooge! a squeezing, wrenching, grasping, scraping, clutching, covetous old sinner! External heat and cold had little influence on him. No warmth could warm, no cold could chill him. No wind that blew was bitterer than he, no falling snow was more intent upon its purpose, no pelting rain less open to entreaty. Foul

weather didn't know where to have him. The heaviest
rain and snow and hail and sleet could boast of the advantage over him in only one respect,—they often
"came down" handsomely, and Scrooge never did.

Nobody ever stopped him in the street to say, with
gladsome looks, "My dear Scrooge, how are you? When
will you come to see me?" No beggars implored him to
bestow a trifle, no children asked him what it was
o'clock, no man or woman ever once in all his life
inquired the way to such and such a place, of Scrooge.
Even the blind men's dogs appeared to know him, and
when they saw him coming on, would tug their owners
into doorways and up courts; and then would wag their
tails as though they said, "No eyes at all is better than
an evil eye, dark master!"

But what did Scrooge care! It was the very thing he
liked. To edge his way along the crowded paths of life,
warning all human sympathy to keep its distance, was
what the knowing ones call "nuts" to Scrooge.

Once upon a time—of all the good days in the year,
upon a Christmas eve—old Scrooge sat busy in his
counting-house. It was cold, bleak, biting, foggy
weather; and the city clocks had only just gone three,
but it was quite dark already.

The door of Scrooge's counting-house was open, that
he might keep his eye upon his clerk, who, in a dismal
little cell beyond, a sort of tank, was copying letters.
Scrooge had a very small fire, but the clerk's fire was so
very much smaller that it looked like one coal. But he
couldn't replenish it, for Scrooge kept the coal-box in
his own room; and so surely as the clerk came in with
the shovel, the master predicted that it would be neces-

sary for them to part. Wherefore the clerk put on his white comforter, and tried to warm himself at the candle; in which effort, not being a man of a strong imagination, he failed.

"A Merry Christmas, uncle! God save you!" cried a cheerful voice. It was the voice of Scrooge's nephew, who came upon him so quickly that this was the first intimation Scrooge had of his approach.

"Bah!" said Scrooge; "humbug!"

"Christmas a humbug, uncle! You don't mean that, I am sure?"

"I do. Out upon merry Christmas! What's Christmas time to you but a time for paying bills without money; a time for finding yourself a year older, and not an hour richer; a time for balancing your books and having every item in 'em through a round dozen of months presented dead against you? If I had my will, every idiot who goes about with 'Merry Christmas' on his lips should be boiled with his own pudding, and buried with a stake of holly through his heart. He should!"

"Uncle!"

"Nephew, keep Christmas in your own way, and let me keep it in mine."

"Keep it! But you don't keep it."

"Let me leave it alone, then. Much good may it do you! Much good it has ever done you!"

"There are many things from which I might have derived good, by which I have not profited, I dare say, Christmas among the rest. But I am sure I have always thought of Christmas time, when it has come round—apart from the veneration due to its sacred origin, if anything belonging to it *can* be apart from that—as a good time; a kind, forgiving, charitable, pleasant time; the only time I know of, in the long calendar of the year, when men and women seem by one consent to open their shut-up hearts freely, and to think of people below them as if they really were fellow-travellers to the grave, and not another race of creatures bound on other journeys. And therefore, uncle, though it has never put a scrap of gold or silver in my pocket, I believe that it *has* done me good, and *will* do me good; and I say, God bless it!"

The clerk in the tank involuntarily applauded.

"Let me hear another sound from *you,*" said Scrooge, "and you'll keep your Christmas by losing your situation! You're quite a powerful speaker, sir," he added, turning to his nephew. "I wonder you don't go into Parliament."

"Don't be angry, uncle. Come! Dine with us to-morrow."

Scrooge said that he would see him—yes, indeed he did. He went the whole length of the expression, and said that he would see him in that extremity first.

"But why?" cried Scrooge's nephew. "Why?"

"Why did you get married?"

"Because I fell in love."

"Because you fell in love!" growled Scrooge, as if that were the only one thing in the world more ridiculous than a merry Christmas. "Good afternoon!"

"Nay, uncle, but you never came to see me before that happened. Why give it as a reason for not coming now?"

"Good afternoon."

"I want nothing from you; I ask nothing of you; why cannot we be friends?"

"Good afternoon."

"I am sorry, with all my heart, to find you so resolute. We have never had any quarrel, to which I have been a party. But I have made the trial in homage to Christmas, and I'll keep my Christmas humour to the last. So A Merry Christmas, uncle!"

"Good afternoon!"

"And A Happy New-Year!"

"Good afternoon!"

His nephew left the room without an angry word, notwithstanding. The clerk, in letting Scrooge's nephew out, had let two other people in. They were portly gentlemen, pleasant to behold, and now stood, with their hats off, in Scrooge's office. They had books and papers in their hands, and bowed to him.

"Scrooge and Marley's, I believe," said one of the gentlemen, referring to his list. "Have I the pleasure of addressing Mr. Scrooge or Mr. Marley?"

"Mr. Marley has been dead these seven years. He died seven years ago, this very night."

"At this festive season of the year, Mr. Scrooge," said the gentleman, taking up a pen, "it is more than usually desirable that we should make some slight provision for the poor and destitute, who suffer greatly at the present time. Many thousands are in want of common necessaries; hundreds of thousands are in want of common comfort, sir."

"Are there no prisons?"

"Plenty of prisons. But under the impression that

they scarcely furnish Christian cheer of mind or body
to the unoffending multitude, a few of us are endeavouring to raise a fund to buy the poor some meat
and drink, and means of warmth. We choose this time,
because it is a time, of all others, when Want is keenly
felt, and Abundance rejoices. What shall I put you
down for?"

"Nothing!"

"You wish to be anonymous?"

"I wish to be left alone. Since you ask me what I
wish, gentlemen, that is my answer. I don't make merry
myself at Christmas, and I can't afford to make idle
people merry. I help to support the prisons and the
workhouses,—they cost enough,—and those who are
badly off must go there."

"Many can't go there; and many would rather die."

"If they would rather die, they had better do it, and
decrease the surplus population."

At length the hour of shutting up the counting-house
arrived. With an ill-will Scrooge, dismounting from his
stool, tacitly admitted the fact to the expectant clerk in
the tank, who instantly snuffed his candle out, and put
on his hat.

"You want all day to-morrow, I suppose?"

"If quite convenient, sir."

"It's not convenient, and it's not fair. If I was to stop
half a crown for it, you'd think yourself mightily ill-
used, I'll be bound?"

"Yes, sir."

"And yet you don't think *me* ill-used, when I pay a
day's wages for no work."

"It's only once a year, sir."

"A poor excuse for picking a man's pocket every twenty-fifth of December! But I suppose you must have the whole day. Be here all the earlier *next* morning."

The clerk promised that he would, and Scrooge walked out with a growl. The office was closed in a twinkling, and the clerk, with the long ends of his white comforter dangling below his waist (for he boasted no great-coat), went down a slide, at the end of a lane of boys, twenty times, in honour of its being Christmas eve, and then ran home as hard as he could pelt to play at blindman's buff.

Scrooge took his melancholy dinner in his usual melancholy tavern; and having read all the newspapers, and beguiled the rest of the evening with his banker's book, went home to bed. He lived in chambers which had once belonged to his deceased partner. They were a gloomy suite of rooms, in a lowering pile of building up a yard. The building was old enough now, and dreary enough, for nobody lived in it but Scrooge, the other rooms being all let out as offices.

Now it is a fact, that there was nothing at all particular about the knocker on the door of this house, except that it was very large; also, that Scrooge had seen it, night and morning, during his whole residence in that place; also, that Scrooge had as little of what is called fancy about him as any man in the city of London. And yet Scrooge, having his key in the lock of the door, saw in the knocker, without its undergoing any intermediate process of change, not a knocker, but Marley's face.

Marley's face, with a dismal light about it, like a bad

lobster in a dark cellar. It was not angry or ferocious, but it looked at Scrooge as Marley used to look— ghostly spectacles turned up upon its ghostly forehead.

As Scrooge looked fixedly at this phenomenon, it was a knocker again. He said, "Pooh, pooh!" and closed the door with a bang.

The sound resounded through the house like thunder. Every room above, and every cask in the wine-merchant's cellars below, appeared to have a separate peal of echoes of its own. Scrooge was not a man to be frightened by echoes. He fastened the door, and walked across the hall, and up the stairs. Slowly too, trimming his candle as he went.

Up Scrooge went, not caring a button for its being very dark. Darkness is cheap, and Scrooge liked it. But before he shut his heavy door, he walked through his rooms to see that all was right. He had just enough recollection of the face to desire to do that.

Sitting-room, bedroom, lumber-room, all as they should be. Nobody under the table, nobody under the sofa; a small fire in the grate; spoon and basin ready; and a little saucepan of gruel (Scrooge had a cold in his head) upon the hob. Nobody under the bed; nobody in the closet; nobody in his dressing-gown, which was hanging up in a suspicious attitude against the wall. Lumber-room as usual. Old fire-guards, old shoes, two fish-baskets, washing-stand on three legs, and a poker.

Quite satisfied, he closed his door, and locked himself in; double-locked himself in, which was not his custom. Thus secured against surprise, he took off his cravat, put on his dressing-gown and slippers and his nightcap, and sat down before the very low fire to take his gruel.

As he threw his head back in the chair, his glance

happened to rest upon a bell, a disused bell, that hung in the room, and communicated, for some purpose now forgotten, with a chamber in the highest story of the building. It was with great astonishment, and with a strange, inexplicable dread, that, as he looked, he saw this bell begin to swing. Soon it rang out loudly, and so did every bell in the house.

This was succeeded by a clanking noise, deep down below as if some person were dragging a heavy chain over the casks in the wine-merchant's cellar.

Then he heard the noise much louder, on the floors below; then coming up the stairs; then coming straight towards his door.

It came on through the heavy door, and a spectre passed into the room before his eyes. And upon its coming in, the dying flame leaped up, as though it cried, "I know him! Marley's ghost!"

The same face, the very same. Marley in his pigtail, usual waistcoat, tights, and boots. His body was transparent; so that Scrooge, observing him, and looking through his waistcoat, could see the two buttons on his coat behind.

Scrooge had often heard it said that Marley had no bowels, but he had never believed it until now.

No, nor did he believe it even now. Though he looked the phantom through and through, and saw it standing before him,—though he felt the chilling influence of its death-cold eyes, and noticed the very texture of the folded kerchief bound about its head and chin,—he was still incredulous.

"How now!" said Scrooge, caustic and cold as ever. "What do you want with me?"

"Much!"—Marley's voice, no doubt about it.

"Who are you?"

"Ask me who I *was*."

"Who *were* you then?"

"In life I was your partner, Jacob Marley."

"Can you—can you sit down?"

"I can."

"Do it, then."

Scrooge asked the question, because he didn't know whether a ghost so transparent might find himself in a condition to take a chair; and felt that, in the event of its being impossible, it might involve the necessity of an embarrassing explanation. But the ghost sat down on the opposite side of the fireplace, as if he were quite used to it.

"You don't believe in me."

"I don't."

"What evidence would you have of my reality beyond that of your senses?"

"I don't know."

"Why do you doubt your senses?"

"Because a little thing affects them. A slight disorder of the stomach makes them cheats. You may be an undigested bit of beef, a blot of mustard, a crumb of cheese, a fragment of an underdone potato. There's more of gravy than of grave about you, whatever you are!"

Scrooge was not much in the habit of cracking jokes, nor did he feel in his heart by any means waggish then. The truth is, that he tried to be smart, as a means of distracting his own attention, and keeping down his horror.

But how much greater was his horror when, the

phantom taking off the bandage round its head, as if it were too warm to wear indoors, its lower jaw dropped down upon its breast!

"Mercy! Dreadful apparition, why do you trouble me? Why do spirits walk the earth, and why do they come to me?"

"It is required of every man that the spirit within him should walk abroad among his fellow-men, and travel far and wide; and if that spirit goes not forth in life, it is condemned to do so after death. I cannot tell you all I would. A very little more is permitted to me. I cannot rest, I cannot stay, I cannot linger anywhere. My spirit never walked beyond our counting-house— mark me!—in life my spirit never roved beyond the narrow limits of our money-changing hole; and weary journeys lie before me!"

"Seven years dead. And travelling all the time? You travel fast?"

"On the wings of the wind."

"You might have got over a great quantity of ground in seven years."

"O blind man, blind man! not to know that ages of incessant labour by immortal creatures for this earth must pass into eternity before the good of which it is susceptible is all developed. Not to know that any Christian spirit working kindly in its little sphere, whatever it may be, will find its mortal life too short for its vast means of usefulness. Not to know that no space of regret can make amends for one life's opportunities misused! Yet I was like this man; I once was like this man!"

"But you were always a good man of business,

Jacob," faltered Scrooge, who now began to apply this to himself.

"Business!" cried the Ghost, wringing its hands again. "Mankind was my business. The common welfare was my business; charity, mercy, forbearance, benevolence, were all my business. The dealings of my trade were but a drop of water in the comprehensive ocean of my business!"

Scrooge was very much dismayed to hear the spectre going on at this rate, and began to quake exceedingly.

"Hear me! My time is nearly gone."

"I will. But don't be hard upon me! Don't be flowery, Jacob! Pray!"

"I am here to-night to warn you that you have yet a chance and hope of escaping my fate. A chance and hope of my procuring, Ebenezer."

"You were always a good friend to me. Thank'ee!"

"You will be haunted by Three Spirits."

"Is that the chance and hope you mentioned, Jacob? I—I think I'd rather not."

"Without their visits, you cannot hope to shun the path I tread. Expect the first to-morrow night, when the bell tolls One. Expect the second on the next night at the same hour. The third, upon the next night, when the last stroke of Twelve has ceased to vibrate. Look to see me no more; and look that, for your own sake, you remember what has passed between us!"

It walked backward from him; and at every step it took, the window raised itself a little, so that, when the apparition reached it, it was wide open.

Scrooge closed the window, and examined the door by which the Ghost had entered. It was double-locked, as he had locked it with his own hands, and the bolts were undisturbed. Scrooge tried to say, "Humbug!" but stopped at the first syllable. And being, from the emotion he had undergone, or the fatigues of the day, or his glimpse of the invisible world, or the dull conversation of the Ghost, or the lateness of the hour, much in need of repose, he went straight to bed, without undressing, and fell asleep on the instant.

Stave Two: THE FIRST OF THE THREE SPIRITS

When Scrooge awoke, it was so dark, that, looking out of bed, he could scarcely distinguish the transparent window from the opaque walls of his chamber, until suddenly the church clock tolled a deep, dull, hollow, melancholy ONE.

Light flashed up in the room upon the instant, and the curtains of his bed were drawn aside by a strange figure,—like a child; yet not so like a child as like an old man, viewed through some supernatural medium, which gave him the appearance of having receded from the view, and being diminished to a child's proportions. Its hair, which hung about its neck and down its back, was white as if with age; and yet the face had not a wrinkle in it, and the tenderest bloom was on the skin. It held a branch of fresh green holly in its hand; and, in singular contradiction of that wintry emblem, had its dress trimmed with summer flowers. But the strangest thing about it was, that from the crown of its head there sprung a bright clear jet of light, by which all this was visible; and which was doubtless the occasion of its using, in its duller moments, a great extinguisher for a cap, which it now held under its arm.

"Are you the Spirit, sir, whose coming was foretold to me?"

"I am!"

"Who and what are you?"

"I am the Ghost of Christmas Past."

"Long Past?"

"No. Your past. The things that you will see with me are shadows of the things that have been; they will have no consciousness of us."

Scrooge then made bold to inquire what business brought him there.

"Your welfare. Rise and walk with me!"

It would have been in vain for Scrooge to plead that the weather and the hour were not adapted to pedestrian purposes; that bed was warm, and the thermometer a long way below freezing; that he was clad but lightly in his slippers, dressing-gown, and night-cap; and that he had a cold upon him at that time. The grasp, though gentle as a woman's hand, was not to be resisted. He rose; but finding that the Spirit made towards the window, clasped its robe in supplication.

"I am a mortal, and liable to fall."

"Bear but a touch of my hand *there*," said the Spirit, laying it upon his heart, "and you shall be upheld in more than this!"

As the words were spoken, they passed through the wall, and stood in the busy thoroughfares of a city. It was made plain enough by the dressing of the shops that here, too, it was Christmas time. The Ghost stopped at a certain warehouse door, and asked Scrooge if he knew it.

"Know it! I was apprenticed here!"

They went in. At sight of an old gentleman in a Welsh wig, sitting behind such a high desk that, if he had been two inches taller, he must have knocked his head against the ceiling, Scrooge cried in great excitement: "Why, it's old Fezziwig! Bless his heart, it's Fezziwig, alive again!"

Old Fezziwig laid down his pen, and looked up at the clock, which pointed at the hour of seven. He rubbed his hands; adjusted his capacious waistcoat; laughed all over himself, from his shoes to his organ of benevolence; and called out in a comfortable, oily, rich, fat, jovial voice: "Yo ho, there! Ebenezer! Dick!"

A living moving picture of Scrooge's former self, a young man, came briskly in, accompanied by his fellow-apprentice.

"Dick Wilkins, to be sure!" said Scrooge to the Ghost. "My old fellow-prentice, bless me, yes. There he is. He was very much attached to me, was Dick. Poor Dick! Dear, dear!"

"Yo ho, my boys!" said Fezziwig. "No more work to-night. Christmas eve, Dick. Christmas, Ebenezer! Let's have the shutters up, before a man can say Jack Robinson! Clear away, my lads, and let's have lots of room here!"

Clear away! There was nothing they wouldn't have cleared away, or couldn't have cleared away, with old Fezziwig looking on. It was done in a minute. Every movable was packed off, as if it were dismissed from public life for evermore; the floor was swept and watered, the lamps were trimmed, fuel was heaped upon the fire; and the warehouse was as snug and warm and dry and bright a ballroom as you would desire to see on a winter's night.

In came a fiddler with a music-book, and went up to the lofty desk, and made an orchestra of it, and tuned like fifty stomach-aches. In came Mrs. Fezziwig, one vast substantial smile. In came the three Miss Fezziwigs, beaming and lovable. In came the six young followers whose hearts they broke. In came all the young men and women employed in the business. In came the housemaid, with her cousin the baker. In came the cook, with her brother's particular friend the milkman. In they all came one after another; some shyly, some boldly, some gracefully, some awkwardly, some pushing, some pulling; in they all came, anyhow and everyhow. Away they all went, twenty couples at once; hands half round and back again the other way; down the middle and up again; round and round in various stages of affectionate grouping; old top couple always turning up in the wrong place; new top couple starting off again, as soon as they got there; all top couples at last, and not a bottom one to help them. When this result was brought about, old Fezziwig, clapping his hands to stop the dance, cried out, "Well done"; and the fiddler plunged his hot face into a pot of porter especially provided for that purpose.

There were more dances, and there were forfeits, and more dances, and there was cake, and there was negus, and there was a great piece of Cold Roast, and there was a great piece of Cold Boiled, and there were mince-pies, and plenty of beer. But the great effect of the evening came after the Roast and Boiled, when the

fiddler struck up "Sir Roger de Coverley." Then old
Fezziwig stood out to dance with Mrs. Fezziwig. Top
couple, too; with a good stiff piece of work cut out for
them; three or four and twenty pair of partners; people
who were not to be trifled with; people who *would*
dance, and had no notion of walking.

But if they had been twice as many—four times—old
Fezziwig would have been a match for them, and so
would Mrs. Fezziwig. As to *her,* she was worthy to be
his partner in every sense of the term. A positive light
appeared to issue from Fezziwig's calves. They shone in
every part of the dance. You couldn't have predicted,
at any given time, what would become of 'em next.
And when old Fezziwig and Mrs. Fezziwig had gone all
through the dance,—advance and retire, turn your
partner, bow and curtsy, corkscrew, thread the needle,
and back again to your place,—Fezziwig "cut,"—cut so
deftly, that he appeared to wink with his legs.

When the clock struck eleven this domestic ball
broke up. Mr. and Mrs. Fezziwig took their stations,
one on either side of the door, and, shaking hands with
every person individually as he or she went out, wished
him or her a Merry Christmas. When everybody had
retired but the two 'prentices, they did the same to
them; and thus the cheerful voices died away, and the
lads were left to their beds, which were under a counter
in the back shop.

"A small matter," said the Ghost, "to make these
silly folks so full of gratitude. He has spent but a few
pounds of your mortal money,—three or four perhaps.
Is that so much that he deserves this praise?"

"It isn't that," said Scrooge, heated by the remark,

and speaking unconsciously like his former, not his latter self,—"it isn't that, Spirit. He has the power to
render us happy or unhappy; to make our service light
or burdensome; a pleasure or a toil. Say that his power
lies in words and looks; in things so slight and insignificant that it is impossible to add and count 'em
up: what then? The happiness he gives is quite as great
as if it cost a fortune."

He felt the Spirit's glance, and stopped.

"What is the matter?"

"Nothing particular."

"Something, I think?"

"No, no. I should like to be able to say a word or two
to my clerk just now. That's all."

"My time grows short," observed the Spirit.
"Quick!"

This was not addressed to Scrooge, or to any one
whom he could see, but it produced an immediate
effect. For again he saw himself. He was older now; a
man in the prime of life.

He was not alone, but sat by the side of a fair young
girl in a black dress, in whose eyes there were tears.

"It matters little," she said softly to Scrooge's former
self. "To you very little. Another idol has displaced me;
and if it can comfort you in time to come, as I would
have tried to do, I have no just cause to grieve."

"What idol has displaced you?"

"A golden one. You fear the world too much. I have
seen your nobler aspirations fall off one by one, until
the master-passion, Gain, engrosses you. Have I not?"

"What then? Even if I have grown so much wiser,

what then? I am not changed towards you. Have I ever sought release from our engagement?"

"In words, no. Never."

"In what, then?"

"In a changed nature; in an altered spirit; in another atmosphere of life; another Hope as its great end. If you were free to-day, tomorrow, yesterday, can even I believe that you would choose a dowerless girl; or, choosing her, do I not know that your repentance and regret would surely follow? I do; and I release you. With a full heart, for the love of him you once were."

"Spirit! remove me from this place."

"I told you these were shadows of the things that have been," said the Ghost. "That they are what they are, do not blame me!"

"Remove me!" Scrooge exclaimed. "I cannot bear it! Leave me! Take me back. Haunt me no longer!"

As he struggled with the Spirit he was conscious of being exhausted, and overcome by an irresistible drowsiness; and, further, of being in his own bedroom. He had barely time to reel to bed before he sank into a heavy sleep.

Stave Three: THE SECOND OF THE THREE SPIRITS

Scrooge awoke in his own bedroom. There was no doubt about that. But it and his own adjoining sitting-room, into which he shuffled in his slippers, attracted by a great light there, had undergone a surprising transformation. The walls and ceiling were so hung with living green, that it looked a perfect grove. The leaves of holly, mistletoe, and ivy reflected back the light, as if so many little mirrors had been scattered there; and such a mighty blaze went roaring up the chimney, as that petrifaction of a hearth had never known in Scrooge's time, or Marley's, or for many and many a winter season gone. Heaped upon the floor, to form a kind of throne, were turkeys, geese, game, brawn, great joints of meat, sucking pigs, long wreaths of sausages, mince-pies, plum-puddings, barrels of oysters, red-hot chestnuts, cherry-cheeked apples, juicy oranges, luscious pears, immense twelfth-cakes, and great bowls of punch. In easy state upon this couch there sat a Giant glorious to see; who bore a glowing torch, in shape not unlike Plenty's horn, and who raised it high to shed its light on Scrooge, as he came peeping round the door.

"Come in,—come in! and know me better, man! I am the Ghost of Christmas Present. Look upon me! You have never seen the like of me before."

"Never."

"Have never walked forth with the younger members of my family; meaning (for I am very young) my elder brothers born in these later years?" pursued the Phantom.

"I don't think I have, I am afraid I have not. Have you had many brothers, Spirit?"

"More than eighteen hundred."

"A tremendous family to provide for! Spirit, conduct me where you will. I went forth last night on compulsion, and I learnt a lesson which is working now. To-night, if you have aught to teach me, let me profit by it."

"Touch my robe!"

Scrooge did as he was told, and held it fast.

The room and its contents all vanished instantly, and they stood in the city streets upon a snowy Christmas morning.

Scrooge and the Ghost passed on, invisible, straight to Scrooge's clerk's; and on the threshold of the door the Spirit smiled, and stopped to bless Bob Cratchit's dwelling with the sprinklings of his torch. Think of that! Bob had but fifteen "bob" a week himself; he pocketed on Saturdays but fifteen copies of his Christian name; and yet the Ghost of Christmas Present blessed his four-roomed house!

Then up rose Mrs. Cratchit, Cratchit's wife, dressed out but poorly in a twice-turned gown, but brave in ribbons, which are cheap and make a goodly show for sixpence; and she laid the cloth, assisted by Belinda Cratchit, second of her daughters, also brave in ribbons; while Master Peter Cratchit plunged a fork into the sauce-pan of potatoes, and, getting the corners of his monstrous shirt-collar (Bob's private property, conferred upon his son and heir in honour of the day) into his mouth, rejoiced to find himself so gallantly attired, and yearned to show his linen in the fashionable Parks. And now two smaller Cratchits, boy and girl, came tearing in, screaming that outside the baker's they had smelt the goose, and known it for their own; and, basking in luxurious thoughts of sage and onion, these young Cratchits danced about the table, and exalted Master Peter Cratchit to the skies, while he (not proud, although his collars nearly choked him) blew the fire, until the slow potatoes, bubbling up, knocked loudly at the saucepan-lid to be let out and peeled.

"What has ever got your precious father then?" said Mrs. Cratchit. "And your brother Tiny Tim! And Martha warn't as late last Christmas day by half an hour!"

"Here's Martha, mother!" said a girl, appearing as she spoke.

"Here's Martha, mother!" cried the two young Cratchits. "Hurrah! There's *such* a goose, Martha!"

"Why, bless your heart alive, my dear, how late you are!" said Mrs. Cratchit, kissing her a dozen times, and taking off her shawl and bonnet for her.

"We'd a deal of work to finish up last night," replied the girl, "and had to clear away this morning, mother!"

"Well! Never mind so long as you are come," said Mrs. Cratchit. "Sit ye down before the fire, my dear, and have a warm, Lord bless ye!"

"No, no! There's father coming," cried the two young Cratchits, who were everywhere at once. "Hide, Martha, hide!"

So Martha hid herself, and in came little Bob, the father, with at least three feet of comforter, exclusive of the fringe, hanging down before him; and his threadbare clothes darned up and brushed, to look seasonable; and Tiny Tim upon his shoulder. Alas for Tiny Tim, he bore a little crutch, and had his limbs supported by an iron frame!

"Why, where's our Martha?" cried Bob Cratchit, looking round.

"Not coming," said Mrs. Cratchit.

"Not coming!" said Bob, with a sudden declension in his high spirits; for he had been Tim's blood-horse all

the way from church, and had come home rampant,—
"not coming upon Christmas day!"

Martha didn't like to see him disappointed, if it were
only in joke; so she came out prematurely from behind
the closet door, and ran into his arms, while the two
young Cratchits hustled Tiny Tim, and bore him off
into the wash-house, that he might hear the pudding
singing in the copper.

"And how did little Tim behave?" asked Mrs. Cratchit, when she had rallied Bob on his credulity, and
Bob had hugged his daughter to his heart's content.

"As good as gold," said Bob, "and better. Somehow
he gets thoughtful, sitting by himself so much, and
thinks the strangest things you ever heard. He told me,
coming home, that he hoped the people saw him in the
church, because he was a cripple, and it might be
pleasant to them to remember, upon Christmas day,
who made lame beggars walk and blind men see."

Bob's voice was tremulous when he told them this,
and trembled more when he said that Tiny Tim was
growing strong and hearty.

His active little crutch was heard upon the floor, and
back came Tiny Tim before another word was spoken,
escorted by his brother and sister to his stool beside the
fire; and while Bob, turning up his cuffs,—as if, poor
fellow, they were capable of being made more shabby,
—compounded some hot mixture in a jug with gin and
lemons, and stirred it round and round, and put it on
the hob to simmer, Master Peter and the two ubiquitous
young Cratchits went to fetch the goose, with which
they soon returned in high procession.

Mrs. Cratchit made the gravy (ready beforehand in

a little saucepan) hissing hot; Master Peter mashed the
potatoes with incredible vigour; Miss Belinda sweet-
ened up the apple-sauce; Martha dusted the hot
plates; Bob took Tiny Tim beside him in a tiny corner
at the table; the two young Cratchits set chairs for everybody, not forgetting themselves, and mounted guard
upon their posts, crammed spoons into their mouths,
lest they should shriek for goose before their turn came
to be helped. At last the dishes were set on, and grace
was said. It was succeeded by a breathless pause, as
Mrs. Cratchit, looking slowly all along the carving-
knife, prepared to plunge it in the breast; but when she
did, and when the long-expected gush of stuffing issued
forth, one murmur of delight arose all round the board,
and even Tiny Tim, excited by the two young Cratchits,
beat on the table with the handle of his knife, and
feebly cried, Hurrah!

There never was such a goose. Bob said he didn't believe there ever was such a goose cooked. Its tenderness
and flavour, size and cheapness, were the themes of
universal admiration. Eked out by apple-sauce and
mashed potatoes, it was a sufficient dinner for the
whole family; indeed, as Mrs. Cratchit said with great
delight (surveying one small atom of a bone upon the
dish) they hadn't ate it all at last! Yet every one had
had enough, and the youngest Cratchits in particular
were steeped in sage and onion to the eyebrows! But
now, the plates being changed by Miss Belinda, Mrs.
Cratchit left the room alone,—too nervous to bear
witnesses,—to take the pudding up, and bring it in.

Suppose it should not be done enough! Suppose it
should break in turning out! Suppose somebody should

have got over the wall of the back yard, and stolen it, while they were merry with the goose,—a supposition at which the two young Cratchits became livid! All sorts of horrors were supposed.

Hallo! A great deal of steam! The pudding was out of the copper. A smell like a washing-day! That was the cloth. A smell like an eating-house and a pastry-cook's next door to each other, with a laundress's next door to that! That was the pudding! In half a minute Mrs. Cratchit entered,—flushed but smiling proudly— with the pudding, like a speckled cannon-ball, so hard and firm, blazing in half of half a quartern of ignited brandy, and bedight with Christmas holly stuck in the top.

Oh, a wonderful pudding! Bob Cratchit said, and calmly too, that he regarded it as the greatest success achieved by Mrs. Cratchit since their marriage. Mrs. Cratchit said that now the weight was off her mind, she would confess she had had her doubts about the quantity of flour. Everybody had something to say about it, but nobody said or thought it was at all a small pudding for a large family. Any Cratchit would have blushed to hint at such a thing.

At last the dinner was all done, the cloth was cleared, the hearth swept, and the fire made up. The compound in the jug being tasted, and considered perfect, apples and oranges were put upon the table, and a shovelful of chestnuts on the fire.

Then all the Cratchit family drew round the hearth, in what Bob Cratchit called a circle, and at Bob Cratchit's elbow stood the family display of glass,—two tumblers, and a custard-cup without a handle.

These held the hot stuff from the jug, however, as
well as golden goblets would have done; and Bob
served it out with beaming looks, while the chestnuts on
the fire spluttered and crackled noisily. Then Bob proposed:—

"A Merry Christmas to us all, my dears. God bless
us!"

Which all the family re-echoed.

"God bless us every one!" said Tiny Tim, the last of
all.

He sat very close to his father's side, upon his little
stool. Bob held his withered little hand in his, as if he
loved the child, and wished to keep him by his side, and
dreaded that he might be taken from him.

Scrooge raised his head speedily, on hearing his own
name.

"Mr. Scrooge!" said Bob; "I'll give you Mr. Scrooge,
the Founder of the Feast!"

"The Founder of the Feast indeed!" cried Mrs.
Cratchit, reddening. "I wish I had him here. I'd give
him a piece of my mind to feast upon, and I hope he'd
have a good appetite for it."

"My dear," said Bob, "the children! Christmas day."

"It should be Christmas day, I am sure," said she,
"on which one drinks the health of such an odious,
stingy, hard, unfeeling man as Mr. Scrooge. You know
he is, Robert! Nobody knows it better than you do,
poor fellow!"

"My dear," was Bob's mild answer, "Christmas
day."

"I'll drink his health for your sake and the day's,"
said Mrs. Cratchit, "not for his. Long life to him! A

merry Christmas and a happy New Year! He'll be very merry and very happy, I have no doubt!"

The children drank the toast after her. It was the first of their proceedings which had no heartiness in it. Tiny Tim drank it last of all, but he didn't care twopence for it. Scrooge was the Ogre of the family. The mention of his name cast a dark shadow on the party, which was not dispelled for full five minutes.

After it had passed away, they were ten times merrier than before, from the mere relief of Scrooge the Baleful being done with. Bob Cratchit told them how he had a situation in his eye for Master Peter, which would bring him, if obtained, full five and sixpence weekly. The two young Cratchits laughed tremendously at the idea of Peter's being a man of business; and Peter himself looked thoughtfully at the fire from between his collars, as if he were deliberating what particular investments he should favour when he came into the receipt of that bewildering income. Martha, who was a poor apprentice at a milliner's, then told them what kind of work she had to do, and how many hours she worked at a stretch, and how she meant to lie abed to-morrow morning for a good long rest; to-morrow being a holiday she passed at home. Also how she had seen a countess and a lord some days before, and how the lord "was much about as tall as Peter"; at which Peter pulled up his collars so high that you couldn't have seen his head if you had been there. All this time the chestnuts and the jug went round and round; and by and by they had a song, about a lost child travelling in the snow, from Tiny Tim, who had a plaintive little voice, and sang it very well indeed.

There was nothing of high mark in this. They were not a handsome family; they were not well dressed; their shoes were far from being waterproof; their clothes were scanty; and Peter might have known, and very likely did, the inside of a pawnbroker's. But they were happy, grateful, pleased with one another, and contented with the time; and when they faded, and looked happier yet in the bright sprinklings of the Spirit's torch at parting, Scrooge had his eye upon them, and especially on Tiny Tim, until the last.

It was a great surprise to Scrooge, as this scene vanished, to hear a hearty laugh. It was a much greater surprise to Scrooge to recognize it as his own nephew's, and to find himself in a bright, dry, gleaming room, with the Spirit standing smiling by his side, and looking at that same nephew.

It is a fair, even-handed, noble adjustment of things, that while there is infection in disease and sorrow, there is nothing in the world so irresistibly contagious as laughter and good-humour. When Scrooge's nephew laughed, Scrooge's niece by marriage laughed as heartily as he. And their assembled friends, being not a bit behindhand, laughed out lustily.

"He said that Christmas was a humbug, as I live!" cried Scrooge's nephew. "He believed it too!"

"More shame for him, Fred!" said Scrooge's niece, indignantly. Bless those women! they never do anything by halves. They are always in earnest.

She was very pretty; exceedingly pretty. With a dimpled, surprised-looking, capital face; a ripe little mouth that seemed made to be kissed,—as no doubt it was; all kinds of good little dots about her chin, that melted into one another when she laughed; and the sunniest pair of eyes you ever saw in any little creature's head. Altogether she was what you would have called provoking, but satisfactory, too. Oh, perfectly satisfactory.

"He's a comical old fellow," said Scrooge's nephew, "that's the truth; and not so pleasant as he might be. However, his offences carry their own punishment, and I have nothing to say against him. Who suffers by his ill whims? Himself, always. Here he takes it into his head to dislike us, and he won't come and dine with us. What's the consequence? He don't lose much of a dinner."

"Indeed, I think he loses a very good dinner," interrupted Scrooge's niece. Everybody else said the same, and they must be allowed to have been competent judges, because they had just had dinner; and, with the dessert upon the table, were clustered round the fire, by lamplight.

"Well, I am very glad to hear it," said Scrooge's nephew, "because I haven't any great faith in these young housekeepers. What do you say, Topper?"

Topper clearly had his eye on one of Scrooge's niece's sisters, for he answered that a bachelor was a wretched outcast, who had no right to express an opinion on the subject. Whereat Scrooge's niece's sister— the plump one with the lace tucker; not the one with the roses—blushed.

After tea they had some music. For they were a musical family, and knew what they were about, when they sung a Glee or Catch, I can assure you,— especially Topper, who could growl away in the bass

like a good one, and never swell the large veins in his
forehead, or get red in the face over it.

But they didn't devote the whole evening to music.
After a while they played at forfeits; for it is good to be
children sometimes, and never better than at Christmas, when its mighty Founder was a child himself.
There was first a game at blindman's buff though. And
I no more believe Topper was really blinded than I believe he had eyes in his boots. Because the way in which
he went after that plump sister in the lace tucker was
an outrage on the credulity of human nature. Knocking down the fire-irons, tumbling over the chairs,
bumping up against the piano, smothering himself
among the curtains, wherever she went there went he!
He always knew where the plump sister was. He
wouldn't catch anybody else. If you had fallen up
against him, as some of them did, and stood there, he
would have made a feint of endeavouring to seize you,
which would have been an affront to your under-
standing, and would instantly have sidled off in the direction of the plump sister.

"Here is a new game," said Scrooge. "One half-hour,
Spirit, only one!"

It was a Game called Yes and No, where Scrooge's
nephew had to think of something, and the rest must
find out what; he only answering to their questions yes
or no, as the case was. The fire of questioning to which
he was exposed elicited from him that he was thinking
of an animal, a live animal, rather a disagreeable animal, a savage animal, an animal that growled and
grunted sometimes, and talked sometimes, and lived in
London, and walked about the streets, and wasn't

made a show of, and wasn't led by anybody, and didn't live in a menagerie, and was never killed in a market, and was not a horse, or an ass, or a cow, or a bull, or a tiger, or a dog, or a pig, or a cat, or a bear. At every new question put to him, this nephew burst into a fresh roar of laughter; and was so inexpressibly tickled, that he was obliged to get up off the sofa and stamp. At last the plump sister cried out:—

"I have found it out! I know what it is, Fred! I know what it is!"

"What is it?" cried Fred.

"It's your uncle Scro-o-o-o-oge!"

Which it certainly was. Admiration was the universal sentiment, though some objected that the reply to "Is it a bear?" ought to have been "Yes."

Uncle Scrooge had imperceptibly become so gay and light of heart, that he would have drank to the unconscious company in an inaudible speech. But the whole scene passed off in the breath of the last word spoken by his nephew; and he and the Spirit were again upon their travels.

Much they saw, and far they went, and many homes they visited, but always with a happy end. The Spirit stood beside sick-beds, and they were cheerful; on foreign lands, and they were close at home; by struggling men, and they were patient in their greater hope; by poverty, and it was rich. In almshouse, hospital, and jail, in misery's every refuge, where vain man in his little brief authority had not made fast the door, and barred the Spirit out, he left his blessing, and taught Scrooge his precepts. Suddenly, as they stood together in an open place, the bell struck twelve.

Scrooge looked about him for the Ghost, and saw it no more. As the last stroke ceased to vibrate, he remembered the prediction of old Jacob Marley, and, lifting up his eyes, beheld a solemn Phantom, draped and hooded, coming like a mist along the ground towards him.

Stave Four: THE LAST OF THE SPIRITS

The Phantom slowly, gravely, silently approached. When it came near him, Scrooge bent down upon his knee; for in the air through which this Spirit moved it seemed to scatter gloom and mystery.

It was shrouded in a deep black garment, which concealed its head, its face, its form, and left nothing of it visible save one outstretched hand. He knew no more, for the Spirit neither spoke nor moved.

"I am in the presence of the Ghost of Christmas Yet to Come? Ghost of the Future! I fear you more than any spectre I have seen. But as I know your purpose is to do me good, and as I hope to live to be another man from what I was, I am prepared to bear you company, and do it with a thankful heart. Will you not speak to me?"

It gave him no reply. The hand was pointed straight before them.

"Lead on! Lead on! The night is waning fast, and it is precious time to me, I know. Lead on, Spirit!"

They scarcely seemed to enter the city; for the city rather seemed to spring up about them. But there they were in the heart of it, on 'Change, amongst the merchants.

The Spirit stopped beside one little knot of business

men. Observing that the hand was pointed to them, Scrooge advanced to listen to their talk.

"No," said a great fat man with a monstrous chin. "I don't know much about it either way. I only know he's dead."

"When did he die?" inquired another.

"Last night, I believe."

"Why, what was the matter with him? I thought he'd never die."

"God knows," said the first, with a yawn.

"What has he done with his money?" asked a red-faced gentleman.

"I haven't heard," said the man with the large chin. "Company, perhaps. He hasn't left it to me. That's all I know. By, by."

Scrooge was at first inclined to be surprised that the Spirit should attach importance to conversation apparently so trivial; but feeling assured that it must have some hidden purpose, he set himself to consider what it was likely to be. It could scarcely be supposed to have any bearing on the death of Jacob, his old partner, for that was Past, and this Ghost's province was the Future.

He looked about in that very place for his own image; but another man stood in his accustomed corner, and though the clock pointed to his usual time of day for being there, he saw no likeness of himself amongst the multitudes that poured in through the Porch. It gave him little surprise, however; for he had been revolving in his mind a change of life, and he thought and hoped he saw his newborn resolutions carried out in this.

They left this busy scene, and went into an obscure part of the town, to a low shop where iron, old rags, bottles, bones, and greasy offal were bought. A grey-haired rascal, of great age, sat smoking his pipe. Scrooge and the Phantom came into the presence of this man, just as a woman with a heavy bundle slunk into the shop. But she had scarcely entered, when another woman, similarly laden, came in too; and she was closely followed by a man in faded black. After a short period of blank astonishment, in which the old man with the pipe had joined them, they all three burst into a laugh.

"Let the charwoman alone to be the first!" cried she who had entered first. "Let the laundress alone to be the second; and let the undertaker's man alone to be the third. Look here, old Joe, here's a chance! If we haven't all three met here without meaning it!"

"You couldn't have met in a better place. You were made free of it long ago, you know; and the other two ain't strangers. What have you got to sell? What have you got to sell?"

"Half a minute's patience, Joe, and you shall see."

"What odds then! What odds, Mrs. Dilber?" said the woman. "Every person has a right to take care of themselves. *He* always did! Who's the worse for the loss of a few things like these? Not a dead man, I suppose."

Mrs. Dilber, whose manner was remarkable for general propitiation, said, "No, indeed, ma'am."

"If he wanted to keep 'em after he was dead, a wicked old screw, why wasn't he natural in his lifetime? If he had been, he'd have had somebody to look after him when he was struck with Death, instead of lying gasping out his last there, alone by himself."

"It's the truest word that ever was spoke, it's a judgment on him."

"I wish it was a little heavier judgment, and it should have been, you may depend upon it, if I could have laid my hands on anything else. Open that bundle, old Joe, and let me know the value of it. Speak out plain. I'm not afraid to be the first, nor afraid for them to see it."

Joe went down on his knees for the greater convenience of opening the bundle, and dragged out a large and heavy roll of some dark stuff.

"What do you call this? Bed-curtains!"

"Ah! Bed-curtains! Don't drop that oil upon the blankets, now."

"*His* blankets?"

"Whose else's do you think? He isn't likely to take cold without 'em, I dare say. Ah! You may look through that shirt till your eyes ache; but you won't find a hole in it, nor a threadbare place. It's the best he had, and a fine one too. They'd have wasted it by dressing him up in it, if it hadn't been for me."

Scrooge listened to this dialogue in horror.

"Spirit! I see, I see. The case of this unhappy man might be my own. My life tends that way, now. Merciful Heaven, what is this!"

The scene had changed, and now he almost touched a bare, uncurtained bed. A pale light, rising in the outer air, fell straight upon this bed; and on it, unwatched, unwept, uncared for, was the body of this plundered unknown man.

"Spirit, let me see some tenderness connected with a death, or this dark chamber, Spirit, will be for ever present to me."

The Ghost conducted him to poor Bob Cratchit's house,—the dwelling he had visited before,—and found the mother and the children seated round the fire.

Quiet. Very quiet. The noisy little Cratchits were as still as statues in one corner, and sat looking up at Peter, who had a book before him. The mother and her daughters were engaged in needlework. But surely they were very quiet!

"'And he took a child, and set him in the midst of them.'"

Where had Scrooge heard those words? He had not dreamed them. The boy must have read them out, as he and the Spirit crossed the threshold. Why did he not go on?

The mother laid her work upon the table, and put her hand up to her face. "The colour hurts my eyes," she said.

The colour? Ah, poor Tiny Tim!

"They're better now again. It makes them weak by candle-light; and I wouldn't show weak eyes to your father when he comes home, for the world. It must be near his time."

"Past it rather," Peter answered, shutting up his book. "But I think he has walked a little slower than he used, these few last evenings, mother."

"I have known him walk with—I have known him walk with Timy Tim upon his shoulder, very fast indeed."

"And so have I," cried Peter. "Often."

"And so have I," exclaimed another. So had all.

"But he was very light to carry, and his father loved

him so, that it was no trouble,—no trouble. And there is your father at the door!"

She hurried out to meet him; and little Bob in his comforter—he had need of it, poor fellow—came in. His tea was ready for him on the hob, and they all tried who should help him to it most. Then the two young Cratchits got upon his knees and laid, each child, a little cheek against his face, as if they said, "Don't mind it, father. Don't be grieved!"

Bob was very cheerful with them, and spoke pleasantly to all the family. He looked at the work upon the table, and praised the industry and speed of Mrs. Cratchit and the girls. They would be done long before Sunday, he said.

"Sunday! You went to-day, then, Robert?"

"Yes, my dear," returned Bob. "I wish you could have gone. It would have done you good to see how green a place it is. But you'll see it often. I promised him that I would walk there on a Sunday. My little, little child! My little child!"

He broke down all at once. He couldn't help it. If he could have helped it, he and his child would have been farther apart, perhaps, than they were.

"Spectre," said Scrooge, "something informs me that our parting moment is at hand. I know it, but I know not how. Tell me what man that was, with the covered face, whom we saw lying dead?"

The Ghost of Christmas Yet to Come conveyed him to a dismal, wretched, ruinous churchyard.

The Spirit stood amongst the graves, and pointed down to One.

"Before I draw nearer to that stone to which you

point, answer me one question. Are these the shadows of the things that Will be, or are they shadows of the things that May be only?"

Still the Ghost pointed downward to the grave by which it stood.

"Men's courses will foreshadow certain ends, to which, if persevered in, they must lead. But if the courses be departed from, the ends will change. Say it is thus with what you show me!"

The Spirit was immovable as ever.

Scrooge crept towards it, trembling as he went; and, following the finger, read upon the stone of the neglected grave his own name—EBENEZER SCROOGE.

"Am *I* that man who lay upon the bed? No, Spirit! Oh no, no! Spirit! hear me! I am not the man I was. I will not be the man I must have been but for this intercourse. Why show me this, if I am past all hope? Assure me that I yet may change these shadows you have shown me by an altered life."

For the first time the kind hand faltered.

"I will honour Christmas in my heart, and try to keep it all the year. I will live in the Past, the Present, and the Future. The Spirits of all three shall strive within me. I will not shut out the lessons that they teach. Oh, tell me I may sponge away the writing on this stone!"

Holding up his hands in one last prayer to have his fate reversed, he saw an alteration in the Phantom's hood and dress. It shrunk, collapsed, and dwindled down into a bedpost.

Yes, and the bedpost was his own. The bed was his

own, the room was his own. Best and happiest of all, the Time before him was his own, to make amends in!

He was checked in his transports by the churches ringing out the lustiest peals he had ever heard.

Running to the window, he opened it, and put out his head. No fog, no mist, no night; clear, bright, stirring, golden day.

"What's to-day?" cried Scrooge, calling downward to a boy in Sunday clothes, who perhaps had loitered in to look about him.

"Eh?"

"What's to-day, my fine fellow?"

"To-day! Why *Christmas day."*

"It's Christmas day! I haven't missed it. Hallo, my fine fellow!"

"Hallo!"

"Do you know the Poulterer's, in the next street but one, at the corner?"

"I should hope I did."

"An intelligent boy! A remarkable boy! Do you know whether they've sold the prize Turkey that was hanging up there? Not the little prize Turkey,—the big one?"

"What, the one as big as me?"

"What a delightful boy! It's a pleasure to talk to him. Yes, my buck!"

"It's hanging there now."

"Is it? Go and buy it."

"Walk-*er!"* exclaimed the boy.

"No, no, I am in earnest. Go and buy it, and tell 'em to bring it here, that I may give them the direction where to take it. Come back with the man, and I'll give you a shilling. Come back with him in less than five minutes, and I'll give you half a crown!"

The boy was off like a shot.

"I'll send it to Bob Cratchit's! He sha'n't know who sends it. It's twice the size of Tiny Tim. Joe Miller never made such a joke as sending it to Bob's will be!"

The hand in which he wrote the address was not a steady one; but write it he did, somehow, and went down stairs to open the street door, ready for the coming of the poulterer's man.

It was a Turkey! He never could have stood upon his legs, that bird. He would have snapped 'em short off in a minute, like sticks of sealing-wax.

Scrooge dressed himself "all in his best," and at last got out into the streets. The people were by this time pouring forth, as he had seen them with the Ghost of Christmas Present; and, walking with his hands behind him, Scrooge regarded every one with a delighted smile. He looked so irresistibly pleasant, in a word, that three or four good-humoured fellows said, "Good morning, sir! A merry Christmas to you!" And Scrooge said often afterwards, that, of all the blithe sounds he had ever heard, those were the blithest in his ears.

In the afternoon, he turned his steps towards his nephew's house.

He passed the door a dozen times, before he had the courage to go up and knock. But he made a dash, and did it.

"Is your master at home, my dear?" said Scrooge to the girl. Nice girl! Very.

"Yes, sir."

"Where is he, my love?"

"He's in the dining-room, sir, along with mistress."

"He knows me," said Scrooge, with his hand already on the dining-room lock. "I'll go in here, my dear."

"Fred!"

"Why, bless my soul!" cried Fred, "who's that?"

"It's I. Your uncle Scrooge. I have come to dinner. Will you let me in, Fred?"

Let him in! It is a mercy he didn't shake his arm off. He was at home in five minutes. Nothing could be heartier. His niece looked just the same. So did Topper when *he* came. So did the plump sister when *she* came. So did every one when *they* came. Wonderful party, wonderful games, wonderful unanimity, won-derful happiness!

But he was early at the office next morning. Oh, he was early there. If he could only be there first, and catch Bob Cratchit coming late! That was the thing he had set his heart upon.

And he did it. The clock struck nine. No Bob. A quarter past. No Bob. Bob was full eighteen minutes and a half behind his time. Scrooge sat with his door wide open, that he might see him come into the tank.

Bob's hat was off before he opened the door; his comforter too. He was on his stool in a jiffy; driving away with his pen, as if he were trying to overtake nine o'clock.

"Hallo!" growled Scrooge, in his accustomed voice, as near as he could feign it. "What do you mean by coming here at this time of day?"

"I am very sorry, sir. I *am* behind my time."

"You are? Yes. I think you are. Step this way if you please."

"It's only once a year, sir. It shall not be repeated. I was making rather merry yesterday, sir."

"Now, I'll tell you what, my friend. I am not going to stand this sort of thing any longer. And therefore," Scrooge continued, leaping from his stool, and giving Bob such a dig in the waistcoat that he staggered back into the tank again,—"and therefore I am about to raise your salary!"

Bob trembled, and got a little nearer to the ruler.

"A merry Christmas, Bob!" said Scrooge, with an earnestness that could not be mistaken, as he clapped him on the back. "A merrier Christmas, Bob, my good fellow, than I have given you for many a year! I'll raise your salary, and endeavour to assist your struggling family, and we will discuss your affairs this very afternoon, over a Christmas bowl of smoking bishop, Bob! Make up the fires, and buy a second coal-scuttle before you dot another *i*, Bob Cratchit!"

Scrooge was better than his word. He did it all, and infinitely more; and to Tiny Tim, who did NOT die, he was a second father. He became as good a friend, as good a master, and as good a man as the good old city knew, or any other good old city, town, or borough in the good old world. Some people laughed to see the alteration in him; but his own heart laughed, and that was quite enough for him.

He had no further intercourse with Spirits, but lived in that respect upon the Total Abstinence Principle ever afterwards; and it was always said of him that he knew how to keep Christmas well, if any man alive possessed the knowledge. May that be truly said of us, and all of us! And so, as Tiny Tim observed, God Bless Us, Every One!

Transition

ALGERNON BLACKWOOD

H. P. Lovecraft, in addition to being the creator of his own strange tales, was also a superb historian of supernatural literature. He considered Algernon Blackwood one of the very greatest writers of spectral literature in this age, or in any age.

Blackwood was able to discover and record the overtones of strangeness in ordinary things and experience. And, as Lovecraft said, he was the one absolute and unquestioned master of weird atmosphere. He was able to evoke a story from the simplest fragment of psychological description, and he knew, above all, how some minds dwell forever on the borderline of dreams, how some souls can transcend the boundaries of life and death.

This extraordinary Christmas story by Algernon Blackwood has another quality he rarely exhibited—a gentle humanity.

JOHN MUDBURY was on his way home from the shops, his arms full of Christmas Presents. It was after six o'clock and the streets were very crowded. He was an ordinary man, lived in an ordinary suburban flat, with an ordinary wife and ordinary children. *He* did not think them ordinary, but everybody else did. He had ordinary presents for each one, a cheap blotter for his wife, a cheap air-gun for the boy, and so forth. He was over fifty, bald, in an office, decent in mind and habits, of uncertain opinions, uncertain politics, and uncertain religion. Yet he considered himself a decided, positive gentleman, quite unaware that the morning newspaper determined his opinions for the day. He just lived— from day to day. Physically, he was fit enough, except for a weak heart (which never troubled him); and his summer holiday was bad golf, while the children bathed and his wife read Garvice on the sands. Like the majority of men, he dreamed idly of the past, muddled away the present, and guessed vaguely—after imaginative reading on occasions—at the future.

"I'd like to survive all right," he said, "provided it's better than this," surveying his wife and children, and thinking of his daily toil. "Otherwise——!" and he shrugged his shoulders as a brave man should.

He went to church regularly. But nothing in church convinced him that he did survive, just as nothing in church enticed him into hoping that he would. On the other hand, nothing in life persuaded him that he didn't, wouldn't, couldn't. "I'm an Evolutionist," he loved to say to thoughtful cronies (over a glass), having never heard that Darwinism had been questioned.

And so he came home gaily, happily, with his bunch

of Christmas Presents "for the wife and little ones,"
stroking himself upon their keen enjoyment and excitement. The night before he had taken "the wife" to see
Magic at a select London theatre where the Intel-
lectuals went—and had been extraordinarily stirred.
He had gone questioningly, yet expecting something
out of the common. "It's *not* musical," he warned her,
"nor farce, no comedy, so to speak"; and in answer to
her question as to what the critics had said, he had
wriggled, sighed, and put his gaudy neck-tie straight
four times in quick succession. For no Man in the
Street, with any claim to self-respect, could be expected
to understand what the critics had said, even if he understood the Play. And John had answered truthfully:
"Oh, they just said things. But the theatre's always full
—and that's the only test."

And just now, as he crossed the crowded Circus to
catch his 'bus, it chanced that his mind (having
glimpsed an advertisement) was full of this particular
Play, or, rather, of the effect it had produced upon him
at the time. For it had thrilled him—inexplicably:
with its marvellous speculative hint, its big audacity, its
alert and spiritual beauty. . . . Thought plunged to
find something—plunged after this bizarre suggestion
of a bigger universe, after this quasi-jocular suggestion
that man is not the only—then dashed full-tilt against a
sentence that memory thrust beneath his nose: "Sci-
ence does *not* exhaust the Universe"—and at the same
time dashed full-tilt against destruction of another kind
as well. . . . !

How it happened he never exactly knew. He saw
a Monster glaring at him with eyes of blazing fire. It

was horrible! It rushed upon him. He dodged. . . .
Another Monster met him round the corner. Both came
at him simultaneously. He dodged again—a leap
that might have cleared a hurdle easily, but was too
late. Between the pair of them—his heart literally
in his gullet—he was mercilessly caught. Bones
crunched. . . . There was a soft sensation, icy cold and
hot as fire. Horns and voices roared. Battering-rams
he saw, and a carapace of iron. . . . Then dazzling
light. . . . "Always *face* the traffic!" he remembered
with a frantic yell—and, by some extraordinary luck,
escaped miraculously on to the opposite pavement.

There was no doubt about it. By the skin of his teeth
he had dodged a rather ugly death. First . . . he felt
for his Presents—all were safe. And then, instead of
congratulating himself and taking breath, he hurried
homewards—on foot, which proved that his mind had
lost control a bit!—thinking only how disappointed the
wife and children would have been if—well, if anything had happened. Another thing he realised, oddly
enough, was that he no longer really loved his wife, but
had only great affection for her. What made him think
of that, Heaven only knows, but he *did* think of it. He
was an honest man without pretence. This came as a
discovery somehow. He turned a moment, and saw the
crowd gathered about the entangled taxi-cabs, police-
men's helmets gleaming in the lights of the shop windows . . . then hurried on again, his thoughts full of
the joy his Presents would give . . . of the scampering
children . . . and of his wife—bless her silly heart!—
eyeing the mysterious parcels. . . .

And, though he never could explain how, he presently stood at the door of the jail-like building that contained his flat, having walked the whole three miles. His thoughts had been so busy and absorbed that he had hardly noticed the length of weary trudge. "Besides," he reflected, thinking of the narrow escape, "I've had a nasty shock. It was a d——d near thing, now I come to think of it. . . ." He still felt a bit shaky and bewildered. Yet, at the same time, he felt extraordinarily jolly and lighthearted.

He counted his Christmas parcels . . . hugged himself in anticipatory joy . . . and let himself in swiftly with his latchkey. "I'm late," he realised, "but when she sees the brown-paper parcels, she'll forget to say a word. God bless the old faithful soul." And he softly used the key a second time and entered his flat on tiptoe. . . . In his mind was the master impulse of that afternoon—the pleasure these Christmas Presents would give his wife and children. . . .

He heard a noise. He hung up hat and coat in the poky vestibule (they never called it "hall") and moved softly towards the parlour door, holding the packages behind him. Only of them he thought, not of himself— of his family, that is, not of the packages. Pushing the door cunningly ajar, he peeped in slyly. To his amazement the room was full of people. He withdrew quickly, wondering what it meant. A party? And without his knowing about it! Extraordinary! . . . Keen disappointment came over him. But, as he stepped back, the vestibule, he saw, was full of people too.

He was uncommonly surprised, yet somehow not surprised at all. People were congratulating him. There was a perfect mob of them. Moreover, he knew them all—vaguely remembered them, at least. And they all knew him.

"Isn't it a game?" laughed someone, patting him on the back. *"They* haven't the least idea . . . !"

And the speaker—it was old John Palmer, the book-keeper at the office—emphasised the "they."

"Not the least idea," he answered with a smile, saying something he didn't understand, yet knew was right.

His face, apparently, showed the utter bewilderment he felt. The shock of the collision had been greater than he realized evidently. His mind was wandering. . . . Possibly! Only the odd thing was—he had never felt so clear-headed in his life. Ten thousand things grew simple suddenly. But, how thickly these people pressed about him, and how—familiarly!

"My parcels," he said, joyously pushing his way across the throng. "These are Christmas Presents I've bought for them." He nodded toward the room. "I've saved for weeks—stopped cigars and billiards and—and several other good things—to buy them."

"Good man!" said Palmer with a happy laugh. "It's the heart that counts."

Mudbury looked at him. Palmer had said an amazing truth, only—people would hardly understand and believe him. . . . Would they?

"Eh?" he asked, feeling stuffed and stupid, muddled somewhere between two meanings, one of which was gorgeous and the other stupid beyond belief.

"If you *please,* Mr. Mudbury, step inside. They are expecting you," said a kindly, pompous voice. And, turning sharply, he met the gentle, foolish eyes of Sir

James Epiphany, a director of the Bank where he worked.

The effect of the voice was instantaneous from long habit.

"They are," he smiled from his heart, and advanced as from the custom of many years. Oh, how happy and gay he felt! His affection for his wife was real. Romance, indeed, had gone, but he needed her—and she needed him. And the children—Milly, Bill, and Jean— he deeply loved them. Life was worth living indeed!

In the room was a crowd, but—an astounding silence. John Mudbury looked round him. He advanced towards his wife, who sat in the corner arm-chair with Milly on her knee. A lot of people talked and moved about. Momentarily the crowd increased. He stood in front of them—in front of Milly and his wife. And he spoke—holding out his packages. "It's Christmas Eve," he whispered shyly, "and I've—brought you something —something for everybody. Look!" he held the packages before their eyes.

"Of course, of course," said a voice behind him, "but you may hold them out like that for a century. They'll *never* see them!"

"Of course they won't. But I love to do the old, sweet thing," replied John Mudbury—then wondered with a gasp of stark amazement why he said it.

"*I* think—" whispered Milly, staring round her.

"Well, what do you think?" her mother asked sharply. "You're always thinking something queer."

"I think," the girl continued dreamily, "that Daddy's already here." She paused, then added with a child's impossible conviction, "I'm sure he is. I *feel* him."

There was an extraordinary laugh. Sir James Epiphany laughed. The others—the whole crowd of them —also turned their heads and smiled. But the mother, thrusting the child away from her, rose up suddenly with a violent start. Her face had turned to chalk. She stretched her arms out—into the air before her. She gasped and shivered. There was anguish in her eyes.

"Look" repeated John, "these are the Presents that I brought."

But his voice apparently was soundless. And, with a spasm of icy pain, he remembered that Palmer and Sir James—some years ago—had died.

"It's magic," he cried, "but—I love you, Jinny—I love you—and—and I have always been true to you— as true as steel. We need each other—oh, can't you see —we go on together—you and I—forever and ever—"

"Think," interrupted an exquisitely tender voice, "don't shout! They can't *hear* you now." And, turning, John Mudbury met the eyes of Everard Minturn, their President of the year before. Minturn had gone down with the *Titanic*.

He dropped his parcels then. His heart gave an enormous leap of joy.

He saw her face—the face of his wife—look through him.

But the child gazed straight into his eyes. She *saw* him.

The next thing he knew was that he heard something tinkling . . . far, far away. It sounded miles below him —inside him—he was sounding himself—all utterly bewildering—like a bell. It *was* a bell.

Milly stooped down and picked the parcels up. Her face shone with happiness and laughter. . . .

But a man came in soon after, a man with a ridicu-

lous, solemn face, a pencil, and a notebook. He wore a
dark blue helmet. Behind him came a string of other
men. They carried something . . . something . . . he
could not see exactly what it was. But, when he pressed
forward through the laughing throng to gaze upon it,
he dimly made out two eyes, a nose, a chin, a deep red
smear, and a pair of folded hands upon an overcoat. A
woman's form fell down upon them then, and he heard
soft sounds of children weeping strangely . . . and
other sounds . . . as of familiar voices laughing . . .
laughing gaily.

"They'll join us presently. It goes like a flash. . . ."

And, turning with great happiness in his heart, he
saw that Sir James had said it, holding Palmer by the
arm as with some natural yet unexpected love of sympathetic friendship.

"Come on," said Palmer, smiling like a man who ac-
cepts a gift in universal fellowship, "let's help 'em.
They'll never understand. . . . Still, we can always
try."

The entire throng moved up with laughter and
amusement. It was a moment of hearty, genuine life at
last. Delight and Joy and Peace were everywhere.

Then John Mudbury realised the truth—that he was
dead.

The Ether Hogs

OLIVER ONIONS

Oliver Onions prefixed his first book with this old Scottish charm against ghosts.

From Ghosties, Ghoulies
and long leggedy beasties
and Things that go Bump in the night—
Good Lord, deliver us!

Onions didn't need such a spell; he could charm any ghost, anywhere. A true master of the fantastic in every way, Oliver Onions was also fascinated by that in-between borderland of the senses where strange messages could be picked up—the world, whose investigation today is one of the studies of paranormal psychology. There is a whole traditional modern literature about strange incidences of telepathy and communication with such modern inconveniences, as they were called a decade or two ago—the radio, the telephone, and even TV. This story falls into that category—a Christmas message from somewhere way out there.

WITH ONE FOOT thrust into an angle to brace himself
against the motion of the ship, the twin telephone-
receivers about his head, and one hand on the transmitting key, while the other hovered over screws and
armatures, the young wireless operator was trying to
get into tune. He had had the pitch, but had either lost
it again, or else something had gone wrong on the ship
from which that single urgent call had come. The pear-
shaped incandescent light made cavernous shadows
under his anxiously drawn brows; it shone harshly on
dials and switchboards, on bells and coils, and milled
screws and tubes; and the whole white-painted room
now heeled slowly over this way, and then steeved as
violently back the other, as the liner rolled to the storm.

The operator seemed to be able to get any ship except the one he wanted. As a keyed-up violin-string an-
swers to tension after tension, or as if a shell held to the
ear should sing, not one Song of the Sea, but a multitude, so he fluctuated through level after level of the
diapason of messges that the installation successively
picked up. They were comically various, had the young
operator's face not been so ghastly anxious and set.
"Merry Christmas . . . the *Doric* . . . buy Erie Rail-
roads . . . Merry Christmas . . . overland from Mar-
seilles . . . closing price copper . . . good night . . .
Merry Christmas"—the night hummed with messages
as a telephone exchange hums; and many decks overhead, and many scores of feet above that again, his own
antennæ described vast loops and arcs in the wintry
sky, and from time to time spoke with a roar that
gashed the night.

But of all the confusion of intercourse about him,

what follows is a Conference that the young wireless operator did *not* hear.

The spirits of the Special Committee on Ethereal Traffic and Right of Way were holding an Extraordinary General Meeting. They were holding it because the nuisance had finally become intolerable. Mortal messages tore great rents through space with such a reckless disregard of the Ethereal Regulations that not a ghost among them was safe. A spectre would be going peacefully about his haunting; there would come one of these radio-telegraphic blasts; and lo, his essence would be shattered into fragments, which could only be reassembled after the hideous racket had passed away.

And by haunting they meant, not merely the old-fashioned terrorizing by means of white sheets and clanking fetters, nor yet only the more modern forms of intimidation that are independent of the stroke of midnight and the crowing of the first cock, but also benigner suggestions—their gentle promptings to the poets of the world, their whispered inspirations to its painters, their care for the integrity of letters, their impulses to kindliness, their spurs to bravery, and, in short, any other noble urging that earth-dwellers know, who give their strength and labour for the unprofitable things they believe without ever having seen them.

A venerable spirit with a faint aura of silver beard still clinging about him spoke.

"I think we are agreed something must be done," he said. "Even now, one of the most amiable junior ghosts of my acquaintance, on his way with a *motif* to a poor, tired musician, was radio'd into flinders, and though his own essence is not permanently harmed, his inspiration was shocked quite out of him, and may never be recovered again."

"That is so," another bore witness. "I happened to be projecting myself not far from the spot, and saw the whole occurrence—poor fellow, he had no chance whatever to escape. It was one of these "directive" messages, as they call them, and no ghost of his grade could have stood up for a moment against it."

"But it is the universal messages, sent out equally in all directions, that are the most serious menace to our state," another urged.

"Quite so. We have a chance of getting out of the way of the directive ones, but the others leave us no escape."

"Look—there goes one now," said another, suddenly pointing; "luckily it's far enough away."

There was an indignant clamour.

"Vandals!" "Huns!" "Hooligans!" "Shame!"

Then a female spirit spoke. It was known that she owed her condition to a motor accident on earth.

"I remember a name the grosser ones used to have for those who exceeded the speed limit in their motorcars. They were called road-hogs. In the same way the creators of these disturbances ought to be called etherhogs."

There was applause at this, which the young wireless operator, still seeking his pitch, mistook for the general radio-commotion about him.

"Yes," the female spirit went on (she had always been a little garrulous under encouragement), "I was afflicted with deafness, and in that horrible instrument they call an Insurance Policy I had to pay an extra premium on that account; dear, dear, the number of times my heart jumped into my mouth as their cars whizzed by!"

But at this point two attendant spirits, whose office it was, gently but firmly "damped" her, that is, merged into her and rarefied her astral coherence; they had heard her story many, many times before. The deliberations continued.

Punitive measures were resolved on. With that the question arose, of whom were they to make an example?

"Take a survey," said the spirit with the aura of silver beard; and a messenger was gone, and immediately back again, with the tidings that at that very moment a young operator, in an admirably susceptible condition of nerves, was seeking to compass a further outrage.

"Good!" said the venerable one, dismissing his minion again. "We have now to decide who shall haunt him. The Chair invites suggestions."

Now the selection of a haunter is always a matter for careful thought. Not every ghost can haunt everybody. Indeed, the superior attenuations have often difficulty in manifesting themselves at all so that in practice a duller spirit becomes their deputy. Thus it is only the less ghostly ghosts we of earth know, those barely yet weaned from the breast of the world, and that is the weakness of haunting from the ghostly point of view. The perfect message must go through the imperfect channel. The great ghosts may plan, but the coarser ones execute.

But as this is not unknown on earth also, we need hardly dwell on it.

Now the Committee had no more redoubtable haunter in certain respects than it had in the spirit of an old Scottish engineer, who had suffered translation in the middle days of steam. True, they had to watch him rather carefully, for he had more than once been suspected of having earthly hankerings and regrets; but that, a demerit in one sense, meant added haunting-efficacy in another, and no less a spirit than Vander-decken himself had recommended him for a certain class of seafaring commission. He was bidden to appear, and his errand was explained to him.

"You understand," they said a little severely when all had been made clear. "Your instructions are definite, remember, and you are not to exceed them."

"Ay, ay, sir," said that blunt ghost. "I kenned sail, and I kenned steam, and I ha' sairved on a cable-ship. Ye canna dae better than leave a' tae me."

There was the ring, at any rate, of sincere intention in his tone, and they were satisfied.

"Very well," said the presiding spirit. "You know where to find him. Be off."

"Ay, ay, sir—dinna fash yersel'—I'll gi'e the laddie a twisting!"

But at that moment a terrific blast from the Cape Cod Station scattered the meeting as if it had been blown from the muzzle of a gun.

And you are to understand that the foregoing took no time at all, as earthly time is reckoned.

II

"Oh, get out of my way, you fool! I want the ship that called me five minutes ago—the *Bainbridge*. Has

she called you? . . . O Lord, here's another lunatic—
wants to know who's won the prizefight! Are you the
Bainbridge? Then buzz off! . . . You there have you
had a call from the *Bainbridge?* Yes, five minutes ago;
I think she said she was on fire, but I'm not sure, and I
can't get her note again! You try—shove that Merry
Christmas fool out—— B-a-i-n . . . No, but I think—I
say I think—she said so—perhaps she can't transmit
any more. . . ."

Dot, dash—dot, dash—dot, dash——

Again he was running up and down the gamut, seeking the ship that had given him that flickering, uncertain message, and then—silence.

A ship on fire—somewhere——

He was almost certain she had said she was on
fire——

And perhaps she could no longer transmit——

Anyway, half a dozen ships were trying for her now.

It was at this moment, when the whole stormy night
throbbed with calls for the *Bainbridge,* that the ghost
came to make an example of the young wireless operator for the warning of Ethereal Trespassers at large.

Indeed, the ships were making an abominable
racket. The Morse tore from the antennae through the
void, and if a homeless spectre missed one annihilating
wavelength he encountered another. They raged. What
was the good of their being the Great Majority if they
were to be bullied by a mortal minority with these
devastating devices at its command?

Even as that ghostly avenger, in a state of imminent
precipitation, hung about the rocking operating-room,
he felt himself racked by disintegrating thrills. The

young operator's fingers were on the transmitting key again.

"Can't you get the *Bainbridge?* Oh, try, for God's sake! . . . Are you there? Nothing come through yet? . . . *Doric.* Can't you couple? . . ."

Lurch, heave; crest, trough; a cant to port, an angle of forty-five degrees to starboard; on the vessel drove, with the antennae high overhead describing those dizzy loops and circles and rending the night with the sputtering Morse.

Dot, dash—dot, dash—dot, dash . . .

But already that old ghost, who in his day had known sail and steam and had served on a cable-ship, had hesitated even on the brink of manifestation. He knew that he was only a low-grade ghost, charged rather than trusted with an errand, and their own evident mistrust of him was not a thing greatly to strengthen his allegiance to them. He began to remember his bones and blood, and his past earthly passion for his job. He had been a fine engineer, abreast of all the knowledge of his day, and what he now saw puzzled him exceedingly. By virtue of his instantaneousness and ubiquity, he had already taken a complete conspectus of the ship. Much that he had seen was new, more not. The engines were more powerful, yet essentially the same. In the stokeholds, down the interminable escalades, all was much as it had formerly been. Of electric lighting he had seen more than the beginnings, so that the staring incandescents were no wonder to him, and on the liner's fripperies of painted and gilded saloons and gymnasium and staterooms and swimming-baths he had wasted little attention. And yet even in gathering himself for visibility he had hesitated. He tried to tell himself why he did so. He told himself that, formidable haunter as he was, it is no easy matter to haunt a deeply preoccupied man. He told himself that he would be able to haunt him all the more soundly did he hold off for awhile and find the hauntee's weak spot. He told himself that his superiors (a little condescending and sniffy always) had after all left a good deal to his discretion. He told himself that, did he return with his errand unaccomplished, they would at all events be no worse off than they had been before.

In a word, he told himself all the things that we mere mortals tell ourselves when we want to persuade ourselves that our inclinations and our consciences are one and the same thing.

And in the meantime he was peering and prying about a little moving band of wires that passed round two wooden pulleys geared to a sort of clock, with certain coils of wire and a couple of horseshoe magnets, the whole attached to the telephone clasped about the young ether-hog's head. He was tingling to know what the thing was for.

It was, of course, the Detector, the instrument's vital ear.

Then the young man's finger began to tap on the transmitter key again.

"*Doric* . . . Anything yet? . . . You're the *Imperator?* . . . Are you calling the *Bainbridge?*"

Now the ghost, who could not make head or tail of the Detector, nevertheless knew Morse; and though it had not yet occurred to him to squeeze himself in between the operator's ears and the telephone receiver, he

read the transmitted message. Also he saw the young
man's strained and sweating face. He wanted some ship
—the *Bainbridge;* from the corrugations of his brows, a
grid in the glare of the incandescent, and the glassy set
of his eyes, he wanted her badly; and so apparently did
those other ships whose mysterious apparatus harrowed
the fields of ether with long and short . . .

Moreover, on board a ship again that wistful old
ghost felt himself at home—or would do so could he
but grasp the operations of that tapping key, of that
air-wire that barked and oscillated overhead, and of
that slowly moving endless band that passed over the
magnets and was attached to the receivers about the
young ether-hog's ears.

Whatever they thought of him who had sent him, he
had been a person of no small account on earth, and a
highly skilled mechanic into the bargain.

Suddenly he found himself in temptation's grip. He
didn't want to haunt this young man. If he did, something might go wrong with that unknown instrument,
and then they might not get this ship they were hunting
through the night.

And if he could only ascertain *why* they wanted her
so badly, it would be the simplest thing in space for a
ghost to find her.

Then, as he nosed about the Detector, it occurred to
him to insinuate a portion of his imponderable fabric
between the receiver and the young man's ear.

The next moment he had started resiliently back
again, as like pole repels like pole of the swinging
needle. He was trembling as no radio-message had ever
set him trembling yet.

Fire! A ship on fire! . . .

That was why these friendly young engineers and operators were blowing a lot of silly ghosts to smithereens! . . .

The *Bainbridge*—on fire! . . .

What did all the ghosts of the universe matter if a ship was on fire?

That faithless emissary did not hesitate for an instant. The ghostly Council might cast him out if they liked; he didn't care; they should be hogged till Doomsday if, on all the seas of the world, a single ship were on fire! A ship on fire? He had once seen a ship on fire, and didn't want, even as a ghost, to see another.

Even while you have been reading this he was off to find the *Bainbridge*.

Of course he hadn't really to go anywhere to find her at all. Low-class and ill-conditioned ghost as he was, he still had that property of ubiquity. An instantaneous double change in his own tension and he was there and back again, with the *Bainbridge*'s bearings, her course, and the knowledge that it was still not too late. The operator was listening in an agony into the twin receivers; a thrill of thankfulness passed through the ghost that he had not forgotten the Morse he had learned on the cable-ship. Swiftly he precipitated himself into a point of action on the transmitter key.

Long, short—long, short—long, short . . .

The operator heard. He started up as if he had been hogged himself. His eyes were staring, his mouth horridly open. What was the matter with his instrument?

Long, short—long, short—long, short . . .

It was not in the telephone. The young man's eyes

fell on his own transmitter key. It was clicking up and down. He read out *"Bainbridge,"* and a bearing, and of course his instrument was spelling it out to the others.

Feverishly he grabbed the telephone.

Already the *Doric* was acknowledging. So was the *Imperator.*

He had sent no message. . . .

Yet, though it made him a little sick to think of it, he would let it stand. If one ship were fooled, all would be fooled. At any rate, he did not think he had dreamed that *first* call, that first horrifying call of *"Bainbridge—* fire!"

He sprang to the tube and called up the bridge.

They picked them up from the *Bainbridge*'s boats towards the middle of Christmas morning; but that unrepentant, old seafaring spectre, returning whence he had come, gave little satisfaction to his superiors. Against all their bullying he was proof; he merely repeated doggedly over and over again, "The laddie's nairves o' steel! Ower and ower again I manifested mysel' tae him, but it made na mair impression on him than if I'd tried to ha'nt Saturn oot o' his Rings! It's my opeenion that being a ghaistie isna what it was. They hae ower mony new-fangled improvements in these days."

But his spectral heart was secretly sad because he had not been able to make head or tail of the Detector.

Christmas Eve in the Blue Chamber

JEROME K. JEROME

*The traditional Christmas ghost appeared in every
magazine issued in December in Britain and the United
States throughout the latter part of the nineteenth century. After a while, such literary fare became almost a
farce. Pathetic ghosts staggered through crumbling
halls till more than one writer felt that the time had
come to say halt.*

*The delightful humorist Jerome K. Jerome was one
of the first to apply his considerable comic gifts to looking askance at these supernatural guests. It was tiresome, indeed, to be approached too often by the uninvited, and although Christmas is a time of enormous
hospitality, there are some ghosts that are too much.
Jerome K. Jerome explores the predicament of a ghost
who hated, yes, hated, Christmas carols sung off key.*

"I DON'T WANT to make you fellows nervous," began
my uncle in a peculiarly impressive, not to say blood-

curdling, tone of voice, "and if you would rather that I did not mention it, I won't; but, as a matter of fact, this very house, in which we are now sitting, is haunted."

"You don't say that!" exclaimed Mr. Coombes.

"What's the use of your saying I don't say it when I have just said it?" retorted my uncle somewhat annoyed. "You talk so foolishly. I tell you the house is haunted. Regularly on Christmas Eve the Blue Chamber," (they call the room next to the nursery the "Blue Chamber" at my uncle's) "is haunted by the ghost of a sinful man—a man who once killed a Christmas carol singer with a lump of coal."

"How did he do it?" asked Mr. Coombes, eagerly. "Was it difficult?"

"I do not know how he did it," replied my uncle; "he did not explain the process. The singer had taken up a position just inside the front gate, and was singing a ballad. It is presumed that, when he opened his mouth for B flat, the lump of coal was thrown by the sinful man from one of the windows, and that it went down the singer's throat and choked him."

"You want to be a good shot, but it is certainly worth trying," murmured Mr. Coombes thoughtfully.

"But that was not his only crime, alas!" added my uncle. "Prior to that he had killed a solo cornet player."

"No! Is that really a fact?" exclaimed Mr. Coombes.

"Of course it's a fact," answered my uncle testily. "At all events, as much a fact as you can expect to get in a case of this sort.

"The poor fellow, the cornet player, had been in the neighborhood barely a month. Old Mr. Bishop, who kept the 'Jolly Sand Boys' at the time, and from whom I had the story, said he had never known a more hard-working and energetic solo cornet player. He, the cornet player, only knew two tunes, but Mr. Bishop said the the man could not have played with more vigor, or for more hours a day, if he had known forty. The two tunes he did play were 'Annie Laurie' and 'Home, Sweet Home'; and as regarded his performance of the former melody, Mr. Bishop said that a mere child could have told what it was meant for.

"This musician—this poor, friendless artist—used to come regularly and play in this street just opposite for two hours every evening. One evening he was seen, evidently in response to an invitation, going into this very house, *but was never seen coming out of it!*"

"Did the townsfolk try offering any reward for his recovery?" asked Mr. Coombes.

"Not a penny," replied my uncle.

"Another summer," continued my uncle, "a German band visited here, intending—so they announced on their arrival—to stay till the autumn.

"On the second day after their arrival, the whole company, as fine and healthy a body of men as one would wish to see, were invited to dinner by this sinful man, and, after spending the whole of the next twenty-four hours in bed, left the town a broken and dyspeptic crew; the parish doctor, who had attended them, giving it as his opinion that it was doubtful if they would, any of them, be fit to play an air again."

"You—you don't know the recipe, do you?" asked Mr. Coombes.

"Unfortunately I do not," replied my uncle; "but the

chief ingredient was said to have been railway dining-room hash.

"I forget the man's other crimes," my uncle went on; "I used to know them all at one time, but my memory is not what it was. I do not, however, believe I am doing his memory an injustice in believing that he was not entirely unconnected with the death, and subsequent burial, of a gentleman who used to play the harp with his toes; and that neither was he altogether unresponsible for the lonely grave of an unknown stranger who had once visited the neighborhood, an Italian peasant lad, a performer upon the barrel-organ.

"Every Christmas Eve," said my uncle, cleaving with low impressive tones the strange awed silence that, like a shadow, seemed to have slowly stolen into and settled down upon the room, "the ghost of this sinful man haunts the Blue Chamber, in this very house. There, from midnight until cock-crow, amid wild muffled shrieks and groans and mocking laughter and the ghostly sound of horrid blows, it does fierce phantom fight with the spirits of the solo cornet player and the murdered carol singer, assisted at intervals by the shades of the German band; while the ghost of the strangled harpist plays mad ghostly melodies with ghostly toes on the ghost of a broken harp."

Uncle said the Blue Chamber was comparatively useless as a sleeping apartment on Christmas Eve.

"Hark!" said my uncle, raising a warning hand toward the ceiling, while we held our breath, and listened: "Hark! I believe they are at it now—in the Blue Chamber!"

I rose up and said that *I* would sleep in the Blue Chamber.

"Never!" cried my uncle, springing up. "You shall not put yourself in this deadly peril. Besides, the bed is not made."

"Never mind the bed," I replied. "I have lived in furnished apartments for gentlemen, and have been accustomed to sleep on beds that have never been made from one year's end to the other. I am young, and have had a clear conscience now for a month. The spirits will not harm me. I may even do them some little good, and induce them to be quiet and go away. Besides, I should like to see the show."

They tried to dissuade me from what they termed my foolhardy enterprise, but I remained firm and claimed my privilege. I was "the guest." "The guest" always sleeps in the haunted chamber on Christmas Eve; it is his right.

They said that if I put it on that footing they had, of course, no answer, and they lighted a candle for me and followed me upstairs in a body.

Whether elevated by the feeling that I was doing a noble action or animated by a mere general consciousness of rectitude is not for me to say, but I went upstairs that night with remarkable buoyancy. It was as much as I could do to stop at the landing when I came to it; I felt I wanted to go on up to the roof. But, with the help of the banisters, I restrained my ambition, wished them all good-night and went in and shut the door.

Things began to go wrong with me from the very

first. The candle tumbled out of the candlestick before
my hand was off the lock. It kept on tumbling out
again; I never saw such a slippery candle. I gave up at-
tempting to use the candlestick at last and carried the
candle about in my hand, and even then it would not
keep upright. So I got wild and threw it out the window, and undressed and went to bed in the dark.

I did not go to sleep; I did not feel sleepy at all; I lay
on my back looking up at the ceiling and thinking of
things. I wish I could remember some of the ideas that
came to me as I lay there, because they were so amus-
ing.

I had been lying like this for half an hour or so, and
had forgotten all about the ghost, when, on casually
casting my eyes round the room, I noticed for the first
time a singularly contented-looking phantom sitting in
the easy-chair by the fire smoking the ghost of a long
clay pipe.

I fancied for the moment, as most people would
under similar circumstances, that I must be dreaming.
I sat up and rubbed my eyes. No! It was a ghost, clear
enough. I could see the back of the chair through his
body. He looked over toward me, took the shadowy
pipe from his lips and nodded.

The most surprising part of the whole thing to me
was that I did not feel in the least alarmed. If anything
I was rather pleased to see him. It was company.

I said: "Good evening. It's been a cold day!"

He said he had not noticed it himself, but dared say I
was right.

We remained silent for a few seconds, and then,
wishing to put it pleasantly, I said: "I believe I have

the honor of addressing the ghost of the gentleman who had the accident with the carol singer?"

He smiled and said it was very good of me to remember it. One singer was not much to boast of, but still every little helped.

I was somewhat staggered at his answer. I had expected a groan of remorse. The ghost appeared, on the contrary, to be rather conceited over the business. I thought that as he had taken my reference to the singer so quietly perhaps he would not be offended if I questioned him about the organ grinder. I felt curious about that poor boy.

"Is it true," I asked, "that you had a hand in the death of that Italian peasant lad who came to the town with a barrel-organ that played nothing but Scotch airs?"

He quite fired up. "Had a hand in it!" he exclaimed indignantly. "Who has dared to pretend that he assisted me? I murdered the youth myself. Nobody helped me. Alone I did it. Show me the man who says I didn't."

I calmed him. I assured him that I had never, in my own mind, doubted that he was the real and only assassin, and I went on and asked him what he had done with the body of the cornet player he had killed.

He said: "To which one may you be alluding?"

"Oh, were there any more then?" I inquired.

He smiled and gave a little cough. He said he did not like to appear to be boasting, but that, counting trombones, there were seven.

"Dear me!" I replied, "you must have had quite a busy time of it, one way and another."

He said that perhaps he ought not to be the one to say so; but that really, speaking of ordinary middle-class society, he thought there were few ghosts who could look back upon a life of more sustained usefulness.

He puffed away in silence for a few seconds while I sat watching him. I had never seen a ghost smoking a pipe before, that I could remember, and it interested me.

I asked him what tobacco he used, and he replied: "The ghost of cut cavendish as a rule."

He explained that the ghost of all the tobacco that a man smoked in life belong to him when he became dead. He said he himself had smoked a good deal of cut cavendish when he was alive, so that he was well supplied with the ghost of it now.

I thought I would join him in a pipe, and he said, "Do, old man"; and I reached over and got out the necessary paraphernalia from my coat pocket and lit up.

We grew quite chummy after that, and he told me all his crimes. He said he had lived next door once to a young lady who was learning to play the guitar, while a gentleman who practiced on the bass-viol lived opposite. And he, with fiendish cunning, had introduced these two unsuspecting young people to one another, and had persuaded them to elope with each other against their parents' wishes, and take their musical instruments with them; and they had done so, and before the honeymoon was over, *she* had broken his head with the bass-viol, and *he* had tried to cram the guitar down her throat, and had injured her for life.

My friend said he used to lure muffin-men into the passage and then stuff them with their own wares till they burst. He said he had quieted eighteen that way.

Young men and women who recited long and dreary poems at evening parties, and callow youths who walked about the streets late at night, playing concertinas, he used to get together and poison in batches of ten, so as to save expenses; and park orators and temperance lecturers he used to shut up six in a small room with a glass of water and a collection-box apiece, and let them talk each other to death.

It did one good to listen to him.

I asked him when he expected the other ghosts—the ghosts of the singer and the cornet player, and the German band that Uncle John had mentioned. He smiled, and said they would never come again, any of them.

I said, "Why, isn't it true, then, that they meet you here every Christmas Eve for a row?"

He replied that it was true. Every Christmas Eve, for twenty-five years, had he and they fought in that room; but they would never trouble him or anybody else again. One by one had he laid them out, spoiled and made them utterly useless for all haunting purposes. He had finished off the last German band ghost that very evening, just before I came upstairs, and had thrown what was left of it out through the slit between the window sashes. He said it would never be worth calling a ghost again.

"I suppose you will still come yourself, as usual?" I said. "They would be sorry to miss you, I know."

"Oh, I don't know," he replied; "there's nothing much to come for now; unless," he added kindly, *"you*

are going to be here. I'll come if you will sleep here
next Christmas Eve."

"I have taken a liking to you," he continued; "you
don't fly off, screeching, when you see a party, and your
hair doesn't stand on end. You've no idea," he said,
"how sick I am of seeing people's hair standing on
end."

He said it irritated him.

Just then a slight noise reached us from the yard
below, and he started and turned deathly black.

"You are ill," I cried, springing toward him; "tell
me the best thing to do for you. Shall I drink some
brandy, and give you the ghost of it?"

He remained silent, listening intently for a moment,
and then he gave a sigh of relief, and the shade came
back to his cheek.

"It's all right," he murmured; "I was afraid it was
the cock."

"Oh, it's too early for that," I said. "Why, it's only
the middle of the night."

"Oh, that doesn't make any difference to those
cursed chickens," he replied bitterly. "They would just
as soon crow in the middle of the night as at any other
time—sooner, if they thought it would spoil a chap's
evening out. I believe they do it on purpose."

He said a friend of his, the ghost of a man who had
killed a tax collector, used to haunt a house in Long
Acre, where they kept fowls in the cellar, and every
time a policeman went by and flashed his searchlight
down the grating, the old cock there would fancy it was
the sun, and start crowing like mad, when, of course,
the poor ghost had to dissolve, and it would, in conse-

quence, get back home sometimes as early as one o'clock in the morning, furious because it had only been out for an hour.

I agreed that it seemed very unfair.

"Oh, it's an absurd arrangement altogether," he continued, quite angrily. "I can't imagine what our chief could have been thinking of when he made it. As I have said to him, over and over again, 'Have a fixed time, and let everybody stick to it—say four o'clock in summer, and six in winter. Then, one would know what one was about.'"

"How do you manage when there isn't any clock handy?" I inquired.

He was on the point of replying, when again he started and listened. This time I distinctly heard Mr. Bowles' cock, next door, crow twice.

"There you are," he said, rising and reaching for his hat; "that's the sort of thing we have to put up with. What *is* the time?"

I looked at my watch, and found it was half-past three.

"I thought as much," he muttered. "I'll wring that blessed bird's neck if I get hold of it." And he prepared to go.

"If you can wait half a minute," I said, getting out of bed, "I'll go a bit of the way with you."

"It's very good of you," he replied, pausing, "but it seems unkind to drag you out."

"Not at all," I replied; "I shall like a walk." And I partially dressed myself, and took my umbrella; and he put his arm through mine, and we went out together, the best of friends.

The White Road

E. F. BOZMAN

The Christmas tree was a latecomer to the decorative festivities of Christmas as we know it in our country. It was introduced to America from Germany, where it had long been a remnant of the splendid and fanciful pageants of the Middle Ages.

Trees, of course, are always contributing lore to magic times—and Christmas, being the most magical time of all, had many trees associated with its importance. The thorn tree of this story and its legends are found in both Britain and the United States. The legend and blossoms flower always on "old Christmas," January 5.

"MILD WEATHER for the time of year."

"Yes," I said; "not very seasonable."

I did not even trouble to turn round and look at the stranger who had addressed me. I remember a soft Sussex voice, strong and deep, and I have an impression of someone tall; but I had come in to have a glass of beer by myself and was not in the mood for chance conversation.

It was Christmas Eve, about nine o'clock in the evening, and the public bar at the Swan Inn was crowded. It was the first evening of my holidays and I had walked over from the farmhouse where I was staying with my mother, using the inn as my objective. I had just come down from London, and was in no need of company; on the contrary, I wanted solitude. However, the landlord recognized me from previous visits and passed the time of night.

"Staying down at the farm again?" he asked.

"Yes," I said.

"Well, we're glad to see you, I'm sure. Did you walk over?"

"Yes. I enjoy the walk. That's what I came out for."

"And for the drink?" he suggested.

"Well, it's good beer," I admitted, and paid for a glass for each of us. I felt rather than saw the stranger who had accosted me hovering behind me, but made no attempt to bring him in. I did not see why I should buy him a drink; and I wanted nothing from him.

"It must be pretty well three miles' walk down to where you are," the landlord said. "A tidy step."

"Yes," I said, "a good three. Two or two and a half down to Ingo Bridge, then another mile from where the lane turns off to West Chapter."

"Well, I suppose you know you've missed the last bus down. Must have gone half an hour. There's only the one in from the Bridge, and that's the lot."

"Yes, I know," I said; "I don't mind."

Just then I heard the noise of the door-latch followed by a creak as the door swung open, and half turned to see the tall stranger going out. I caught a glimpse of him before he shut the door behind him.

"Who was that?" I asked the landlord.

"I didn't notice him—he must have been a stranger to me. Funny thing, now you mention it, he didn't buy a drink."

"He seemed to be hanging round me. Cadging, I suppose."

"You get some funny customers at this time of year." The landlord was evidently not interested in the man. "It'll be dark to-night, along that road," he volunteered.

"Yes," I said. We finished our drinks, I said good night, and made my way to the door across the smoke-laden room.

It was pitch dark outside by contrast with the glow of the inn, and as I slammed the well-used wooden door behind me the shaft of light streaming from the parlour window seemed to be my last link with civilization. The air was extraordinarily mild for the time of year. My way lay by a short cut across the church fields which joined the road leading towards the sea; a difficult way to find at night had I not known it well; alternatively, I could have gone a long way round, starting in the opposite direction, and making three sides of a square in the road which I was eventually to join by the short cut. I knew my ground and decided on the footpath without hesitation. By the time I reached the church fields I realized that the night was not really so dark as it had seemed to be at first, for I could see the black tower and belfry of the church looming against a background of lighter grey, and a glimmer of light in one corner of the church suggested eleventh-hour preparations for the great festival. Clouds were scudding across an unseen moon, full according to the calendar, discernible now only secondarily by a patch of faintly diffused light towards the south; knowing the lie of the land I could imagine the clouds swept away and the moon hanging in its winter glory over the cold English Channel a few miles away. Although the air was temporarily muggy with the presage of rain, there was a deep underlying chill in land and sea, the in-grained coldness of the short days.

The footpath across the fields was narrow and muddy, a single-file track. I stumbled and slithered my way along it until I reached a narrow wooden bridge with two handrails. Here I paused for a moment, look-ing at the dark swollen stream which was just visible, black and shining, below my feet.

I was now near the point where the path joined the road, and as I paused, my elbows leaning on the rail of the bridge, listening to the far-reaching silence, I heard in the distance the sound of footsteps along the road. In these days of heavy road-traffic this old-fashioned, un-mistakable sound is a rarity, and I listened fascinated. The steady distant tread, gradually loudening, began to grow on me, and by the time I had made up my mind to move it was beating a rhythm in my brain. My path now led diagonally up a sloping bank to the road, and I crept up it silently, hearing and thinking of nothing but the approaching footsteps. The thought occurred to me that I must not let the walker catch me up, that something important, something connected with myself yet out of my own control, depended on the success of my efforts, and I began to hurry. I tried to dismiss the idea, but it would not be banished, and as I reached the swing-gate leading out to the road the footsteps sounded unexpectedly near. They rang on the road, and I could hardly resist the temptation to run.

I compromised by stepping out briskly, swinging my arms. It was ludicrous, I argued with myself; there was nothing to be afraid of, and my own feet tried to reassure me by dimming the sound behind me. But the pursuing footsteps would not be drowned; they were implacable. I attempted to speed up, without allowing myself to hurry or panic, but I could not shake them off. They were gaining steadily on me, and as their loudness increased tingles of fear began to go down my spine. I could not turn round and look—could not, I realized, because I was afraid to.

The road at this point runs between high hedges and trees which shut out what little light was coming from the sky. Nothing could be seen except the dark shapes of the trees, and an occasional gleam from the black wet surface of the tarred road. There were some outlying farm buildings and barns immediately ahead, but no glimmer of light came from them. The overhanging elms dripped their moisture on me from leafless branches. No traffic was within earshot; the only sound was of footsteps, mine and my pursuer's.

Left right, left right, left right they went behind me. The walker had long legs. Left right, left right—the din increased alarmingly, and I realized that I must run.

"How far now to the bridge?"

A soft voice, almost in my ear, shocked me, and yet released the tension. I sweated suddenly and profusely.

I recognized the voice of the stranger who had addressed me in the Swan Inn. He had left just before me, I realized, and must have walked round by the road while I had taken the short cut across the fields. I could not immediately disguise my racing heart, but I managed to speak calmly, in a voice which must have sounded weak in contrast with the strong Sussex resonance of the stranger.

"About two miles," I said.

The stranger said nothing more for the moment, but fell into step beside me, as if assuming that we were to walk together. It was not what I wanted, partly because I was ashamed of my panic of a few moments ago, and partly because I had been looking forward to walking the lonely stretch of road ahead by myself. I turned my head, but could see nothing of my dark companion except his tall dark form, vaguely outlined, and he must have been wearing a long coat which flapped below his knees. I was the next to break the silence.

"When we get past the farm buildings," I said, "and round the next corner we come to a long open stretch. It's a lovely bit of road, a special favourite of mine, absolutely deserted usually. On clear nights or days you can see the sea in the distance."

"There's a little hill about half-way along—by an S bend."

The stranger's remark surprised me. Why had he asked me about the way if he knew the district?

"So you know the road?" I asked querulously, as if I had been deceived.

The stranger muttered "Years ago," and something

else I could not catch. The detail he had remembered
was a significant one. The open stretch ahead of us,
nearly two miles in length, promised at first sight to run
straight for the sea, where it joined the main coast
road; but half-way along this section of the road there
was a danger spot for speeding motorists, an unexpected S bend over a little mound. Just past the bend,
as the road straightened itself out again and went down
the far side of the little hill, heading between low
hedges for the sea, there was a notable isolated thorn
tree standing on the left of the road. Its trunk leant towards the sea, while the twigs on top of the trunk were
all swept in the opposite direction, like a mat of hair,
blown by the prevailing wind. From the trunk two
stumpy branches sprouted, each with its bunch of twigs
held out like hands; these, too, were windswept. The
trunk was not gnarled and sprang strongly from the
ground—no dead post, driven into the earth from
above, could have achieved that appearance of
strength.

I was about to refer to this tree, which was a particular landmark of mine, when we heard the sound of a
distant motor. My companion seemed to be unexpectedly nervous—I could feel his anxiety. The sound
increased rapidly, so different a progress from approaching feet, and before we had rounded the sharp
corner leading to the open stretch of road a Southdown
bus flung itself round the bend and was almost on us.
The headlights flooded us, gleaming on the stranger's
face, making him look pale as a ghost, and lighting the
road immediately in front of us to a brilliant white.

The stranger was so dazzled by the sudden brightness

that he cowered into the hedge, shielding his eyes with his hand. In an instant the bus had charged past us and round another corner, taking its lighted interior and its warm passengers with it into the enveloping darkness of the countryside.

I heard my companion murmur, "The white road. The white road." Something in the way he said the words brought a picture of my youth to my eyes, of a time when this same lonely road was white and dusty, with flints, and I could see myself bicycling along it, in imminent danger of punctures, hurrying to the sea. I saw the white road, the white sea road, not the black and tarred contrivance of to-day, yet the same road with the same trees and banks. It has always been a lovely country road, and it still is.

We left the farm buildings behind us and entered the lonely stretch. It was too dark for us to see a glimmer of the sea ahead or anything behind the low banked hedges on either side. A light rain began to fall, driving in our faces.

"That was the last bus," I said, "we'll meet no more now."

The stranger ignored this remark, and his next words fitted in exactly with what had been in my mind when the bus distracted us.

"There's a thorn tree, isn't there?" he said, "just beside the road round the double corner." He spoke as if he knew the way by heart, yet obviously he did not remember it exactly. He had not even been sure enough of himself to take the short cut by the church fields.

"Yes," I said, "why do you ask?"

"You've noticed it yourself?" he inquired anxiously.

"Yes."

"And it's still there?"

"Yes, of course." I could not for the life of me imagine what he was driving at. Yet even as I spoke the words confidently I found myself in doubt. I remembered my mother saying something about workmen on the lonely road, how they were widening it at the bend and spoiling its appearance. Like me, she had an affection for it. I had passed the spot that very evening on my way to the inn, yet when I came to think of it I could not be sure whether I had seen the tree or not. I had been preoccupied, and had not looked for it specially. But surely I would have noticed, I thought, and said aloud, "At least it was there the last time I passed."

"When was that?" The stranger spoke very directly and forcibly.

I was about to say this very evening, but realizing my uncertainty, said instead, "About this time last year. I was down here for Christmas."

"There's a story told about that tree in these parts," he said.

"Oh," I said; "what do they say about it?"

"They say there was a suicide on that spot. A man from the village." The Sussex burr was soft and confidential.

"What happened?"

"He hanged himself on the tree."

"A man couldn't hang himself on that tree," I said, "it's too small."

"There's a seven-foot clearance from the fork," he said eagerly.

"Oh, well," I said, "it's a sturdy little tree. I've often noticed it, standing there all alone, holding out its branches like hands."

"Yes," he said, "that's right. Like hands. And have you seen the nails? Long and curved. They haven't been cut, any more than the hair. Have you seen the hair?" His voice was strained, and I felt he must be looking at me. I turned to read his eyes, but it was too dark to see anything but the tall shape and the long coat beside me.

"That tree didn't grow in a day," I said.

"I don't know how old it is." The stranger spoke apologetically. "But it's an old story—maybe twenty, thirty, forty years old. I couldn't be sure."

There was a pause for a few minutes. We must have covered half the mile between the farm and the tree before I spoke again.

"What's behind the story?" I asked, "what do they say?"

"They say there was a woman in it. A dark girl, one of the coastguard's daughters down at Ingo Bridge. He was a married man, you see."

I waited for him to go on. He spoke as if it mattered vitally to him.

"It had been going on a long time, they say. Then one night, one Christmas Eve, he left his home for good and went to the inn, and perhaps he had a drink or two there, though nobody knows that. He had made up his mind to take the girl. She was going to leave a light burning in her window, and he would see it from the distance, you see, when he turned the corner by the tree. That was to be the sign, if it was all right. Well, he left his home for good, to get that girl. But he never got her. His wife got him—by that tree."

"I thought you said it was suicide."

"Ah, yes, that's what they say. But it was his wife that got him."

"You mean she followed him?"

"No, I mean that she got him there."

We walked another two hundred yards before he added, "I mean that he saw her there, in his mind's eye. He couldn't take the girl then. He couldn't, however much he wanted to. He couldn't because he belonged to his wife. That's what I mean when I say his wife got him."

"It's a queer story," I said, "I've never heard it told before."

"Oh, you hear it among the older men. It's common knowledge," he said.

"It's a queer story," I said, "because who told it in the first place? Who was to know what was in the fellow's mind? Who was to know what actually happened?"

"He was dead, wasn't he?" the stranger spoke irritably. "A man doesn't die in these parts without talk about it. A lot of talk."

"But how did he die?" I insisted. "Did he hang himself or was he murdered?"

"He was murdered."

"What the devil do you mean?" I shouted angrily. "Murdered, by a tree?"

The stranger clutched me by the arm. "Have you seen the tree?" he whispered, "have you seen it standing there year after year, leaning against the south-west

wind, with the hair streaming and the hands outstretched, and the long nails growing——?"

I was suddenly aware of the loneliness of the road
and of the darkness and desolation of the downs around
me and the sea ahead. The stranger's next remark,
though spoken in a low voice, seemed to shatter the
darkness.

"By God! what's a man to do when a woman pulls at
him. A dark girl. And what do men have daughters for,
eh? I ask you that. Whose fault is that?" and then, as if
brushing aside an imaginary criticism, "If I were to
meet that coastguard's daughter down by the bridge to-
night I'd tell her . . ."

His voice tailed off and I said nothing. The coastguards' cottages are still down by the bridge, true
enough, but the coastguards have been disbanded years
ago. Years ago. He must have known that.

We reached the little hill in the road, mounted it,
and turned the first half of the S bend. The light rain
had ceased and the clouds were thinning. We both of us
knew that when we passed the next corner, the other
half of the S, we should see the tree.

Just then the clouds broke suddenly and the full
moon shone through. It whitened the black road, sil-
vered the gleam of the sea ahead, and illuminated the
low banks and hedges with the dark rising downs beyond. We turned the corner and both stared towards
the thorn tree.

There was nothing to be seen. No tree. Nothing. The
place where the tree had stood was blatantly empty,
and the moonlight seemed to emphasize the barrenness,
showing it up like a sore, focusing the attention. I sup-

pose I had been unconsciously visualizing the tree as I
knew it, because I was more than surprised by its absence; I was shocked, profoundly shocked, and the recollection of that absence of tree, that nothingness, is
more vivid to me than my memory of the tree itself. The
clouds now scudded from the moon, leaving it cold and
clear and agonizingly circular in an expanse of sky. In
what seemed to be a blaze of light I put my head down
and ran.

I ran towards the silver sea along a white road, a rib-
bon road of memory, and I could believe that the dust
rose under my feet and powdered my boots; though
with another part of me I knew that I was wearing
shoes, not boots, and was pounding down a wet tarred
road. In the moonlight that road seemed white and
dusty and I pattered along it with the desperate ur-
gency of a small boy who must deliver some message or
run some errand of overwhelming yet not-understood
importance. I ran and I ran, urgently and desperately,
thinking no more of my strange companion, yet in some
way intimately associated with him.

Along the white road I ran, past the signpost at my
own corner, knowing yet not knowing what I should
see. The clouds had gathered again, a dark pillar over
the sea, and the blaze of whiteness was already dimming. There was a light in the coastguard's cottage at
Ingo Bridge. I headed straight for it but did not reach
it, for a woman lay across the road, an elderly woman.
She must have dropped her basket as she fell, for her
parcels, little objects and toys that she had bought for
her grandchildren perhaps, lay scattered around her.

She might have been shopping for Christmas, I thought, and missed the last bus at Ingo Bridge; then she had tried to walk home, but her strength had failed her, and she had fallen in the road.

I ran to her side and raised her head. She was too weak to stand on her feet, and I lifted her in my arms and carried her the few yards to the coastguard's cottage where the light was still burning. For those few steps the road was white and flinty—but then it is so now; it is only a little by-road—and I found myself speaking not to an old woman who had fainted or was dying, but to a young woman. And the words I spoke were not mine but someone else's; the words of the stranger who had accompanied me to the tree. They were framed without my help.

"That was no murder. That was no murder by the tree. I always belonged to you, all along, really. I see it all now."

The woman opened her eyes and there was an expression of love in them. I could not say whether it was I or my stranger who spoke the next words. They were said very gently and comfortably.

"There are things better left unsaid. Better left; you understand."

She nodded and closed her eyes, and then the stranger and the strangeness left me.

I knocked at the door of the cottage. A man opened it, then called to his wife, a grey-haired woman dressed in black, who must have been a beautiful dark girl in her time. I explained what had happened and they

took my burden from me and laid her on their horse-
hair sofa. They knew who she was, of course, for she
was from the village.

But I did not know. I could only guess. And as I
walked back in the inky blackness of an oncoming rain-
storm, back to my corner, then up the lane to the farmhouse where my mother was waiting up for me, I cast
round in my mind for a missing fragment of knowledge, something I must know yet could not remember.

I discovered it at last accidentally, while in my
mind's eye I could still see the thorn tree, standing
there, holding out its branches, its mat of twigs all set
towards the north-east, and from the fork a dark form
hung, twisting slowly in a long coat, a thing with a back
to its head but no face, a dark thing twisting slowly beside a long white road which stretched in a dusty rib-
bon to the sea. I discovered the missing fragment of
knowledge in the more exact recollection of my
mother's remark, made only that very morning. "They
are widening the white road at the bend," she had said
—we always used to call it the white road between ourselves—"and they are going to cut down that little old
thorn tree."

The Necklace of Pearls

DOROTHY L. SAYERS

Decorations for the winter solstice, the Christmas holidays, are familiar to every country and to every time. The Druids hung the mistletoe; we still hang mistletoe and holly today.

Dorothy Sayers, a famous medievalist as well as a great detective writer, had a passion for Christmas. She decorates glitteringly the final pages of this book with a story about Lord Peter Wimsey. His famous hobby of collecting not only criminals but also antiquarian knowledge would have allowed him to join us in an old farewell:

> Well-a-day! well-a-day!
> Christmas too soon goes away.
> > We cannot stay,
> > But must away,
> For the Christmas will not stay,
> Well-a-day! well-a-day!

SIR SEPTIMUS SHALE was accustomed to assert his authority once in the year and once only. He allowed his young and fashionable wife to fill his house with diagrammatic furniture made of steel; to collect advanced artists and anti-grammatical poets; to believe in cocktails and relativity and to dress as extravagantly as she pleased; but he did insist on an old-fashioned Christmas. He was a simple-hearted man, who really liked plum-pudding and cracker mottoes, and he could not get it out of his head that other people, "at bottom," enjoyed these things also. At Christmas, therefore, he firmly retired to his country house in Essex, called in the servants to hang holly and mistletoe upon the cubist electric fittings; loaded the steel sideboard with delicacies from Fortnum & Mason; hung up stockings at the heads of the polished walnut bedsteads; and even, on this occasion only, had the electric radiators removed from the modernist grates and installed wood fires and a Yule log. He then gathered his family and friends about him, filled them with as much Dickensian good fare as he could persuade them to swallow, and, after their Christmas dinner, set them down to play "Charades" and "Clumps" and "Animal, Vegetable, and Mineral" in the drawing-room, concluding these diversions by "Hide-and-Seek" in the dark all over the house. Because Sir Septimus was a very rich man, his guests fell in with this invariable programme, and if they were bored, they did not tell him so.

Another charming and traditional custom which he followed was that of presenting to his daughter Margharita a pearl on each successive birthday—this anniversary happening to coincide with Christmas Eve.

The pearls now numbered twenty, and the collection was beginning to enjoy a certain celebrity, and had been photographed in the Society papers. Though not sensationally large—each one being about the size of a marrow-fat pea—the pearls were of very great value. They were of exquisite colour and perfect shape and matched to a hair's-weight. On this particular Christmas Eve, the presentation of the twenty-first pearl had been the occasion of a very special ceremony. There was a dance and there were speeches. On the Christmas night, following, the more restricted family party took place, with the turkey and the Victorian games. There were eleven guests, in addition to Sir Septimus and Lady Shale and their daughter, nearly all related or connected to them in some way: John Shale, a brother, with his wife and their son and daughter Henry and Betty; Betty's fiancé, Oswald Truegood, a young man with parliamentary ambitions; George Comphrey, a cousin of Lady Shale's, aged about thirty and known as a man about town; Lavinia Prescott, asked on George's account; Joyce Trivett, asked on Henry Shale's account; Richard and Beryl Dennison, distant relations of Lady Shale, who lived a gay and expensive life in town on nobody precisely knew what resources; and Lord Peter Wimsey, asked, in a touching spirit of unreasonable hope, on Margharita's account. There were also, of course, William Norgate, secretary to Sir Septimus, and Miss Tomkins, secretary to Lady Shale, who had to be there because, without their calm efficiency, the Christmas arrangements could not have been carried through.

Dinner was over—a seemingly endless succession of

soup, fish, turkey, roast beef, plum-pudding, mince-
pies, crystallized fruit, nuts, and five kinds of wine,
presided over by Sir Septimus, all smiles, by Lady
Shale, all mocking deprecation, and by Margharita,
pretty and bored, with the necklace of twenty-one
pearls gleaming softly on her slender throat. Gorged
and dyspeptic and longing only for the horizontal position, the company had been shepherded into the drawing-room and set to play "Musical Chairs" (Miss
Tomkins at the piano), "Hunt the Slipper" (slipper
provided by Miss Tomkins), and "Dumb Crambo"
(costumes by Miss Tomkins and Mr. William Norgate). The back drawing-room (for Sir Septimus clung
to these old-fashioned names) provided an admirable
dressing-room, being screened by folding doors from
the large drawing-room in which the audience sat on
aluminum chairs, scrabbling uneasy toes on a floor of
black glass under the tremendous illumination of elec-
tricity reflected from a brass ceiling.

It was William Norgate who, after taking the tem-
perature of the meeting, suggested to Lady Shale that
they should play at something less athletic. Lady Shale
agreed and, as usual, suggested bridge. Sir Septimus, as
usual, blew the suggestion aside.

"Bridge? Nonsense! Nonsense! Play bridge every day
of your lives. This is Christmas time. Something we can
all play together. How about 'Animal, Vegetable, and
Mineral'?"

This intellectual pastime was a favourite with Sir
Septimus; he was rather good at putting pregnant
questions. After a brief discussion, it became evident
that this game was an inevitable part of the pro-

gramme. The party settled down to it, Sir Septimus undertaking to "go out" first and set the thing going.

Presently they had guessed among other things Miss Tomkins's mother's photograph, a gramophone record of "I want to be happy" (much scientific research into the exact composition of records, settled by William Norgate out of the *Encyclopaedia Britannica*), the smallest stickleback in the stream at the bottom of the garden, the new planet Pluto, the scarf worn by Mrs. Dennison (very confusing, because it was not silk, which would be animal, or artificial silk, which would be vegetable, but made of spun glass—mineral, a very clever choice of subject), and had failed to guess the Prime Minister's wireless speech—which was voted not fair, since nobody could decide whether it was animal by nature or a kind of gas. It was decided that they should do one more word and then go on to "Hide-and-Seek." Oswald Truegood had retired into the back room and shut the door behind him while the party discussed the next subject of examination, when suddenly Sir Septimus broke in on the argument by calling to his daughter:

"Hullo, Margy! What have you done with your necklace?"

"I took it off, Dad, because I thought it might get broken in 'Dumb Crambo.' It's over here on this table. No, it isn't. Did you take it, mother?"

"No, I didn't. If I'd seen it, I should have. You are a careless child."

"I believe you've got it yourself, Dad. You're teasing."

Sir Septimus denied the accusation with some en-

ergy. Everybody got up and began to hunt about.
There were not many places in that bare and polished
room where a necklace could be hidden. After ten minutes' fruitless investigation, Richard Dennison, who
had been seated next to the table where the pearls had
been placed, began to look rather uncomfortable.

"Awkward, you know," he remarked to Wimsey.

At this moment, Oswald Truegood put his head
through the folding-doors and asked whether they
hadn't settled on something by now, because he was
getting the fidgets.

This directed the attention of the searchers to the
inner room. Margharita must have been mistaken. She
had taken it in there, and it had got mixed up with the
dressing-up clothes somehow. The room was ransacked.
Everything was lifted up and shaken. The thing began
to look serious. After half an hour of desperate energy
it became apparent that the pearls were nowhere to be
found.

"They must be somewhere in these two rooms, you
know," said Wimsey. "The back drawing-room has no
door and nobody could have gone out of the front
drawing-room without being seen. Unless the windows—"

No. The windows were all guarded on the outside by
heavy shutters which it needed two footmen to take
down and replace. The pearls had not gone out that
way. In fact, the mere suggestion that they had left the
drawing-room at all was disagreeable. Because—
because—

It was William Norgate, efficient as ever, who coldly
and boldly, faced the issue.

"I think, Sir Septimus, it would be a relief to the minds of everybody present if we could all be searched."

Sir Septimus was horrified, but the guests, having found a leader, backed up Norgate. The door was locked, and the search was conducted—the ladies in the inner room and the men in the outer.

Nothing resulted from it except some very interesting information about the belongings habitually carried about by the average man and woman. It was natural that Lord Peter Winsey should possess a pair of forceps, a pocket lens, and a small folding foot-rule—was he not a Sherlock Holmes in high life? But that Oswald Truegood should have two liver-pills in a screw of paper and Henry Shale a pocket edition of *The Odes of Horace* was unexpected. Why did John Shale distend the pockets of his dress-suit with a stump of red sealing-wax, an ugly little mascot, and a five-shilling piece? George Comphrey had a pair of folding scissors, and three wrapped lumps of sugar, of the sort served in restaurants and dining-cars—evidence of a not uncommon form of kleptomania; but that the tidy and exact Norgate should burden himself with a reel of white cotton, three separate lengths of string, and twelve safety-pins on a card seemed really remarkable till one remembered that he had superintended all the Christmas decorations. Richard Dennison, amid some confusion and laughter, was found to cherish a lady's garter, a powder-compact, and half a potato; the last-named, he said, was a prophylactic against rheumatism (to which he was subject), while the other objects belonged to his wife. On the ladies' side, the more striking exhibits were a little book on palmistry, three invisible hairpins, and a baby's photograph (Miss Tomkins) ; a Chinese trick cigarette-case with a secret compartment (Beryl Dennison) ; a *very* private letter and an outfit for mending stocking-ladders (Lavinia Prescott) ; and a pair of eyebrow tweezers and a small packet of white powder, said to be for headaches (Betty Shale). An agitating moment followed the production from Joyce Trivett's handbag of a small string of pearls—but it was promptly remembered that these had come out of one of the crackers at dinner-time, and they were, in fact, synthetic. In short, the search was unproductive of anything beyond a general shamefacedness and the discomfort always produced by undressing and re-dressing in a hurry at the wrong time of the day.

It was then that somebody, very grudgingly and haltingly, mentioned the horrid word "Police." Sir Septimus, naturally, was appalled by the idea. It was disgusting. He would not allow it. The pearls must be somewhere. They must search the rooms again. Could not Lord Peter Wimsey, with his experience of—er—mysterious happenings, do something to assist them?

"Eh?" said his lordship. "Oh, by Jove, yes—by all means, certainly. That is to say, provided nobody supposes—eh, what? I mean to say, you don't know that I'm not a suspicious character, do you, what?"

Lady Shale interposed with authority.

"We don't think *anybody* ought to be suspected," she said, "but, if we did, we'd know it couldn't be you. You know *far* too much about crimes to want to commit one."

"All right," said Wimsey. "But after the way the

place has been gone over—" He shrugged his shoulders.

"Yes, I'm afraid you won't be able to find any footprints," said Margharita. "But we may have overlooked something."

Wimsey nodded.

"I'll try. Do you all mind sitting down on your chairs in the outer room and staying there. All except one of you—I'd better have a witness to anything I do or find. Sir Septimus—you'd be the best person, I think."

He shepherded them to their places and began a slow circuit of the two rooms, exploring every surface, gazing up to the polished brazen ceiling, and crawling on hands and knees in the approved fashion across the black and shining desert of the floors. Sir Septimus followed, staring when Wimsey stared, bending with his hands upon his knees when Wimsey crawled, and puffing at intervals with astonishment and chagrin. Their progress rather resembled that of a man taking out a very inquisitive puppy for a very leisurely constitutional. Fortunately, Lady Shale's taste in furnishing made investigation easier; there were scarcely any nooks or corners where anything could be concealed.

They reached the inner drawing-room, and here the dressing-up clothes were again minutely examined, but without result. Finally, Wimsey lay down flat on his stomach to squint under a steel cabinet which was one of the very few pieces of furniture which possessed short legs. Something about it seemed to catch his attention. He rolled up his sleeve and plunged his arm into the cavity, kicked convulsively in the effort to reach farther than was humanly possible, pulled out from his pocket and extended his folding foot-rule, fished with it under the cabinet, and eventually succeeded in extracting what he sought.

It was a very minute object—in fact, a pin. Not an ordinary pin, but one resembling those used by entomologists to impale extremely small moths on the setting-board. It was about three-quarters of an inch in length, as fine as a very fine needle, with a sharp point and a particularly small head.

"Bless my soul!" said Sir Septimus. "What's that?"

"Does anybody here happen to collect moths or beetles or anything?" asked Wimsey, squatting on his haunches and examining the pin.

"I'm pretty sure they don't," replied Sir Septimus. "I'll ask them."

"Don't do that." Wimsey bent his head and stared at the floor, from which his own face stared meditatively back at him.

"I see," said Wimsey presently. "That's how it was done. All right, Sir Septimus. I know where the pearls are, but I don't know who took them. Perhaps it would be as well—for everybody's satisfaction—just to find out. In the meantime they are perfectly safe. Don't tell anyone that we've found this pin or that we've discovered anything. Send all these people to bed. Lock the drawing-room door and keep the key, and we'll get our man—or woman—by breakfast-time."

"God bless my soul," said Sir Septimus, very much puzzled.

Lord Peter Wimsey kept careful watch that night upon the drawing-room door. Nobody, however, came near it. Either the thief suspected a trap or he felt confident that any time would do to recover the pearls. Wimsey, however, did not feel that he was wasting his time. He was making a list of people who had been left alone in the back drawing-room during the playing of "Animal, Vegetable, and Mineral." The list ran as follows:

Sir Septimus Shale
Lavinia Prescott
William Norgate
Joyce Trivett and Henry Shale (together, because they had claimed to be incapable of guessing anything unaided)
Mrs. Dennison
Betty Shale
George Comphrey
Richard Dennison
Miss Tomkins
Oswald Truegood

He also made out a list of the persons to whom pearls might be useful or desirable. Unfortunately, this list agreed in almost all respects with the first (always excepting Sir Septimus) and so was not very helpful. The two secretaries had both come well recommended, but that was exactly what they would have done had they come with ulterior designs; the Dennisons were notorious livers from hand to mouth; Betty Shale carried mysterious white powders in her handbag, and was known to be in with a rather rapid set in town; Henry was a harmless dilettante, but Joyce Trivett could twist him round her little finger and was what Jane Austen liked to call "expensive and dissipated"; Comphrey speculated; Oswald Truegood was rather frequently present at Epsom and Newmarket—the search for motives was only too fatally easy.

When the second housemaid and the under-footman appeared in the passage with household implements, Wimsey abandoned his vigil, but he was down early to breakfast. Sir Septimus with his wife and daughter were down before him, and a certain air of tension made itself felt. Wimsey, standing on the hearth before the fire, made conversation about the weather and politics.

The party assembled gradually, but, as though by common consent, nothing was said about pearls until after breakfast, when Oswald Truegood took the bull by the horns.

"Well now!" said he. "How's the detective getting along? Got your man, Wimsey?"

"Not yet," said Wimsey easily.

Sir Septimus, looking at Wimsey as though for his cue, cleared his throat and dashed into speech.

"All very tiresome," he said, "all very unpleasant. Hr'rm. Nothing for it but the police, I'm afraid. Just at Christmas, too. Hr'rm. Spoilt the party. Can't stand seeing all this stuff about the place." He waved his hand towards the festoons of evergreens and coloured paper that adorned the walls. "Take it all down, eh, what? No heart in it. Hr'rm. Burn the lot."

"What a pity, when we worked so hard over it," said Joyce.

"Oh, leave it, Uncle," said Henry Shale. "You're bothering too much about the pearls. They're sure to turn up."

"Shall I ring for James?" suggested William Norgate.

"No," interrupted Comphrey, "let's do it ourselves. It'll give us something to do and take our minds off our troubles."

"That's right," said Sir Septimus. "Start right away. Hate the sight of it."

He savagely hauled a great branch of holly down from the mantelpiece and flung it, crackling, into the fire.

"That's the stuff," said Richard Dennison. "Make a good old blaze!" He leapt up from the table and snatched the mistletoe from the chandelier. "Here goes! One more kiss for somebody before it's too late."

"Isn't it unlucky to take it down before the New Year?" suggested Miss Tomkins.

"Unlucky be hanged. We'll have it all down. Off the stairs and out of the drawing-room too. Somebody go and collect it."

"Isn't the drawing-room locked?" asked Oswald.

"No. Lord Peter says the pearls aren't there, wherever else they are, so it's unlocked. That's right, isn't it, Wimsey?"

"Quite right. The pearls were taken out of these rooms. I can't tell yet how, but I'm positive of it. In fact, I'll pledge my reputation that wherever they are, they're not up there."

"Oh, well," said Comphrey, "in that case, have at it! Come along, Lavinia—you and Dennison do the drawing-room and I'll do the back room. We'll save a race."

"But if the police are coming in," said Dennison, "oughtn't everything to be left just as it is?"

"Damn the police!" shouted Sir Septimus. "They don't want evergreens."

Oswald and Margharita were already pulling the holly and ivy from the staircase, amid peals of laughter. The party dispersed. Wimsey went quietly upstairs and into the drawing-room, where the work of demolition was taking place at a great rate, George having bet the other two ten shillings to a tanner that they would not finish their part of the job before he finished his.

"You mustn't help," said Lavinia, laughing to Wimsey. "It wouldn't be fair."

Wimsey said nothing, but waited till the room was clear. Then he followed them down again to the hall, spluttering, suggestive of Guy Fawkes' night. He whispered to Sir Septimus, who went forward and touched George Comphrey on the shoulder.

"Lord Peter wants to say something to you, my boy," he said.

Comphrey started and went with him a little reluctantly, as it seemed. He was not looking very well.

"Mr. Comphrey," said Wimsey, "I fancy these are some of your property." He held out the palm of his hand, in which rested twenty-two fine, small-headed pins.

"Ingenious," said Wimsey, "but something less ingenious would have served his turn better. It was very unlucky, Sir Septimus, that you should have mentioned the pearls when you did. Of course, he hoped that the loss wouldn't be discovered till we'd chucked guessing games and taken to "Hide-and-Seek." The pearls might have been anywhere in the house, we shouldn't have locked the drawing-room door, and he could have recovered them at his leisure. He had had this possibility in his mind when he came here, obviously, and that was why he brought the pins, and Miss Shale's taking off the necklace to play "Dumb Crambo" gave him his opportunity.

"He had spent Christmas here before, and knew perfectly well that "Animal, Vegetable, and Mineral" would form part of the entertainment. He had only to gather up the necklace from the table when it came to his turn to retire, and he knew he could count on at least five minutes by himself while we were all arguing about the choice of a word. He had only to snip the pearls from the string with his pocket-scissors, burn the string in the grate, fasten the pearls to the mistletoe with the fine pins. The mistletoe was hung on the chandelier, pretty high—it's a lofty room—but he could easily reach it by standing on the glass table, which wouldn't show footmarks, and it was almost certain that nobody would think of examining the mistletoe for extra berries. I shouldn't have thought of it myself if I hadn't found that pin which he had dropped. That gave me the idea that the pearls had been separated and the rest was easy. I took the pearls off the mistletoe last night—the clasp was there, too, pinned among the holly-leaves. Here they are. Comphrey must have got a nasty shock this morning. I knew he was our man when he suggested that the guests should tackle the decorations themselves and that he should do the back drawing-room—but I wish I had seen his face when he came to the mistletoe and found the pearls gone."

"And you worked it all out when you found the pin?" said Sir Septimus.

"Yes; I knew then where the pearls had gone to."

"But you never even looked at the mistletoe."

"I saw it reflected in the black glass floor, and it struck me then how much the mistletoe berries looked like pearls."

MARJORIE BOWEN, one of the pen names of Gabrielle Margaret Campbell Long, the English novelist, playwright, and biographer, was born at Hayling Island, Hampshire, in 1888. She also wrote under the names of George R. Preedy and Joseph Shearing. Her first novel was published when she was sixteen years old. Altogether she wrote more than a hundred books in fluent and easy style and with great fertility of invention. She died in 1952.

MARGERY ALLINGHAM, British writer, was born in London, England, in 1904, the daughter of Herbert John Allingham, a writer. She started writing at the age of seven and produced her first published novel at sixteen. From then on until her death in 1966, she produced suspense and detective novels which earned her an international reputation. Her husband, Philip Youngman Carter, always discussed her work with her and completed her last book after her death.

EDWARD JOHN MORETON DRAX PLUNKETT, 18th Baron Dunsany, poet and playwright, was born in London in 1878. Educated at Eton and Sandhurst, he succeeded to the title on his father's death in 1899. He served in the Boer War and was wounded in World War I. In World War II he held the chair of Byron Professor of English Literature at Athens, and barely escaped capture by the Germans. By contrast with his work, which consists of delicate fantasies, he was an extremely athletic person; he once estimated that 97 per cent of his time was spent in sport and soldiering, the rest in writing. His first book was a novel, *The Gods of Pegana* (1905); other novels are *Time and the Gods* (1913), *The King of Elfland's Daughter* (1924), and *The Curse of the Wise Woman* (1933). In 1909, on Yeats' invitation, he wrote a play, *The Glittering Gate,* for the Abbey Theater, and followed it with many others. He also published two volumes of verse and a series of autobiographies. He died in 1957.

GRANT ALLEN, scientific writer and novelist, was born in 1848 in Canada, to which his father, a clergyman, had emigrated. He was educated at Birmingham and Oxford. For a time he taught school in Jamaica, but returning to England in 1876 devoted himself to writing. He wrote many books and articles on scientific subjects, but was also interested in fiction and between 1884 and 1899 produced about thirty novels. Later he was attracted to the short story and contributed ghost stories to *Belgravia* and the *Cornhill* magazine. *Strange Stories* (1884) and *The Beckoning Hand* (1887) are collections of his supernatural tales. He died in 1899.

HUGH WALPOLE, novelist, was born in Auckland, New Zealand, in 1884. He was the eldest of the three children of the Reverend George Henry Somerset Walpole, later to become Bishop of Edinburgh. Walpole was educated at King's School, Canterbury, and Cambridge. For a time he was a teacher, then worked as a book reviewer. His first novel, *The Wooden Horse* (1909), was followed by *Maradick at Forty* (1910) and *Mr. Perrin and Mr. Traill* (1911), a study of a teacher's life which some consider his best work. During World War I he served with the Red Cross in Russia, received the Order of St. George, and was made a C.B.E. Russia is the background of his novels *The Dark Forest* (1916) and *The Secret City* (1919). His most ambitious work, *The Herries Chronicle,* a novelized family history, was published in the early nineteen-thirties. He was knighted in 1937 and died in 1941.

CHARLES DICKENS, one of the world's greatest novelists, was born in England in 1812. The son of a navy clerk, he grew up in London. During one of his father's imprisonments for debt, the twelve-year-old Charles was apprenticed in a blacking warehouse and learned firsthand the horror of child labor. At seventeen he became a court shorthand reporter and subsequently a parliamentary reporter for the London *Morning Chronicle*. His sketches of London types (signed "Boz") began appearing in periodicals in 1833, and the collected *Sketches by Boz* (1836) enjoyed a great success. *The Posthumous Papers of the Pickwick Club* (1836–37) made Dickens and his characters Sam Weller and Mr. Pickwick famous. For his eager and ever more numerous readers Dickens worked vigorously, publishing, first in monthly installments and then as books, *Oliver Twist* (1838), *Nicholas Nickleby* (1839), *The Old Curiosity Shop* (1841). He often worked on more than one novel at a time. After a visit to America in 1842, he wrote *American Notes* (1842) and *Martin Chuzzlewit* (1844), both sharply criticizing America's shortcomings. His many other novels, of which *David Copperfield* was his own favorite, were written while he was lecturing, managing his amateur theatrical company, and editing successively two magazines, *Household Words* and *All the Year Round*. He died in 1870 at the age of fifty-eight.

ALGERNON BLACKWOOD, novelist, born in Kent in 1869, son of Sir Author Blackwood and Sydney, Duchess of Manchester, was educated at Wellington and Edinburgh University. At the age of twenty he went to Canada, where he was successively journalist, dairy farmer, hotelkeeper, prospector, artist's model, actor, and private secretary. He had a great interest in the occult and has been called "the Ghost Man" because of his subjects. After two volumes of short stories, *The Empty House* (1906) and *The Listener* (1907), he made his reputation with the weird *John Silence* (1908). Other novels were *The Human Chord* (1910), *The Wave* (1916), and *Dudley and Gilderoy* (1929). *Incredible Adventures* (1914), *Tongues of Fire* (1924), and *Tales of the Uncanny and Supernatural* (1949) are collections of short stories. He wrote several children's books, and the non-fiction *Episodes Before Thirty* (1923), which tells of his early roving life. He died in 1951.

OLIVER ONIONS, novelist, born at Bradford, England, in 1873, changed his name in later life to George Oliver, but always wrote under the name Oliver Onions. He studied art in London and Paris, and worked for a time as an illustrator and designer; in later years he designed his own book jackets. His first book was *The Compleat Bachelor* (1901), but his first real success was with the trilogy of novels *In Accordance with the Evidence* (1912), *The Debit Account* (1913), and *The Story of Louie* (1913). He also wrote highly effective ghost stories, collected in *Widdershins* (1911), *Ghosts in Daylight* (1924), and *The Painted Face* (1929). He died in 1961.

JEROME K. JEROME, English humorist, was born in 1859 in Staffordshire, England, and died in 1927. During his lifetime he worked as a schoolmaster, actor, and finally as a journalist. In 1888 he published his first book. He had a genuine gift for highlighting the more ridiculous aspects of the society of his day, but always with tolerance and a style of humor that owed much to Dickens and Mark Twain. In 1889 he became popular as a writer with *Idle Thoughts of an Idle Fellow* and his most famous book, *Three Men in a Boat*, which sold over a million copies in America.

E. F. (ERNEST FRANKLIN) BOZMAN, English writer and publisher, was born in 1895. He saw active service in World War I (for which he received the Military Cross) and then took a degree at Cambridge University. In 1921 he entered publishing and remained in that profession for forty-five years. In 1926 he was appointed Editorial Director of the old established London firm of J. M. Dent & Sons, a responsibility he retained until his retirement in 1965 and which enabled him to foster many new writers, among them Dylan Thomas. He was the author of three novels and a contributor to various collections of short stories. He died in 1968.

DOROTHY LEIGH SAYERS, writer of detective stories, was born at Oxford, where her father was a headmaster. Educated at Somerville College, she was one of the first women to get an Oxford degree. Her first detective story, *Whose Body?*, was published in

1923, and introduced her now famous young nobleman detective, Lord Peter Wimsey, modeled on one of the more popular dons of her day. In addition to her original work, she is known throughout the world for her three anthologies, *Omnibuses of Crime* (in England, *Great Short Stories of Detection, Mystery, and Horror*). She also wrote a number of plays. Miss Sayers died in 1957.

SEON MANLEY and GOGO LEWIS, who have worked together on many books, are sisters and have been collecting supernatural stories throughout their lives. Mrs. Manley lives in Greenwich, Connecticut, with her management consultant husband Robert, their daughter Shivuan, two dogs, and five supernatural cats.

Mrs. Lewis lives in Bellport, Long Island, where the mist comes in from the bay with all the atmosphere of a Dickens novel. Her daughters, Carol and Sara, are also devotees of the supernatural tale.